Thoroughbred Legacy
The stakes are high.

Scandal has hit the Preston family and their
award-winning Quest Stables. Find out what it will take to
return this horse-racing dynasty to the winner's circle!

Available July 2008

#1 *Flirting with Trouble* by Elizabeth Bevarly
Publicist Marnie Roberts has just been handed a PR disaster,
one that will bring her face-to-face with the man who walked
out of her bed and out of her life eight years ago.

#2 *Biding Her Time* by Wendy Warren
Somehow, Audrey Griffin's motto of "seize the day" has
unexpectedly thrown her into the arms of a straitlaced Aussie
who doesn't do no-strings-attached. Is Audrey balking at
commitment…or simply biding her time?

#3 *Picture of Perfection* by Kristin Gabriel
When Carter Phillips sees an exquisite painting that could be
the key to saving his career, he goes after the artist. Will he
sacrifice his professional future for a personal one with her?

#4 *Something to Talk About* by Joanne Rock
Widowed single mom Amanda Emory is on the run from her
past, but when she meets Quest's trainer she suddenly wants to
risk it all…and give everyone something to talk about!

Dear Reader,

Like most young girls, I loved horses. I recall once attempting to convince my parents that a small stable would fit perfectly in our suburban backyard. Nixing that idea, they opened our home to a number of rescued dogs and cats, and I didn't revisit horses until this book project came along.

The research was fascinating. I learned about horse racing, yes, but also about the bold and complex men, women and animals at the heart of the sport. Bold and complex describes the story line of THOROUGHBRED LEGACY, as a matter of fact, and getting to know the other authors was a pleasure. I hope you enjoy *Biding Her Time* and that it whets your appetite for the books to follow!

Wendy Warren

Thoroughbred Legacy

BIDING
HER TIME

Wendy Warren

Silhouette Books

Published by Silhouette Books
America's Publisher of Contemporary Romance

SILHOUETTE BOOKS

ISBN-13: 978-0-373-19915-0
ISBN-10:   0-373-19915-5

BIDING HER TIME

Special thanks and acknowledgment are given to Wendy Warren
for her contribution to the Thoroughbred Legacy series.

Visit Silhouette Special Edition and Thoroughbred Legacy
at www.eHarlequin.com.

Printed in U.S.A.

WENDY WARREN

lives with her husband and daughter in the beautiful Pacific Northwest. Their house was previously owned by a woman named Cinderella, who bequeathed them a garden full of flowers they try desperately (and occasionally successfully) not to kill, and a pink General Electric oven, circa 1958, that makes the kitchen look like an *I Love Lucy* rerun.

A two-time recipient of the Romance Writers of America's RITA® Award, Wendy loves to read and write the kind of books that remind her of the old movies she grew up watching with her mom—stories about decent people looking for the love that can make an ordinary life heroic. When not writing, she likes to take long walks, hide out in bookstores with her friends and sneak tofu into her husband's dinner. If you'd like a tofu recipe—and who wouldn't?—visit her Web site, www.wendywarren-author.com.

With deep gratitude to the editors,
past and present, who have taught me to write
and paid me to do it.

From the early years: Wendy Corsi Staub,
Anne Canadeo and Lynda Curnyn.

Susan Litman, my current editor,
is savvy, talented, smart as a whip and sends e-mails
that knock me off my chair with laughter.

Stacy Boyd and Marsha Zinberg invited me on-board
the Thoroughbred Legacy project and have guided it
surely and with terrific grace.

I am very appreciative!

Chapter One

"Put your hands in your pockets, boys, and dig deep. I'm about to lighten your loads."

Bending over a pool table that had seen more money change hands than Chase Manhattan Bank, Audrey Griffin stretched one toned, well-muscled arm along the green felt. Loose auburn waves spilled over her shoulder as she cocked her opposite elbow back and lined up a seemingly impossible shot.

"Thirteen in the corner," she called, then sank the ball so fast, a few of the men around the table cussed a blue streak guaran*damn*teed to set their mamas to praying.

Laying her cue stick atop the well-used table, Audrey brushed her hands, shrugged and let an obnoxious grin spread over her face. "Anyone for darts?"

Colby Dale told her what would have to happen to hell before he played *anything* with her *ever* again, but he tossed her a ten spot before walking away. Two of the others coughed up handfuls of dollar bills, and Jed Clooney gave her two bucks in change plus an IOU, just to be irritating.

"Aw, c'mon." Audrey gathered her winnings, patting the cash into a neat pile. "I've been beating y'all since Red Bullet won the Preakness. You gotta be used to it by now."

"You've been gloating about it that long, too," Jed reminded her as he gathered up cue sticks, "and we're not used to *that* yet." But he tweaked Audrey's nose as he passed by to show there were no hard feelings. "Nice game, junior. The old man would be proud."

Audrey felt tears well up.

Shit.

Blinking the emotion away, she pushed her smile higher. No way would she lose it now. Not when she'd been sucking it up successfully all day.

"Beer! I'm buying." Leading the procession to the bar, she ordered ten Michelob drafts from Herman, the proprietor of Hot to Trot, added shots for those who wanted them and raised her jigger of bourbon immediately when it came. "Live for today, for tomorrow we may die," she toasted, trying to remember if there was more to the quote, then deciding it was fine just as it stood.

The boys must have agreed with her, because every shot glass bottomed up along with hers. The glasses returned to the bar with a clunk, warm hands reached for icy beers, and talk turned to a couple of local yearlings that had graduated from the Keeneland spring sale in April.

As the conversation heated up along the mahogany and tufted-leather bar, Audrey relinquished her stool and stepped away from the others. The guys would be content to nurse their beers and talk horses the rest of the night, but she didn't have the focus right now to discuss business. Nor did she have the desire to chase her whiskey with beer. It felt better tonight, or at least more appropriate, to let the eighty-proof Kentucky bourbon have its way with her—burning the back of her throat, threading her veins with a thin coil of heat that made her feel uncomfortably weak. Patting the base of her throat, where the alcohol stung, she decided that bourbon and life had a lot in common: fun in the moment, but you had to be prepared for consequences.

Antsy, Audrey glanced around the room and spied the jukebox. Music. That's what she needed tonight—and not the sticky *Peyton Place* theme currently playing, either. Slipping away to feed the machine, she chose her songs, then faced Hot To Trot's scuffed square of a dance floor, her gaze flicking toward the bar.

A couple of women with whom she'd gone to high school had joined the group of men, scooting their jeans-clad, teeny tiny tushies onto bar stools already occupied by a jockey and a groom from Quest, the same stable at which she worked. Each woman had one superslender arm flung around the neck of the man whose seat she shared, probably to avoid falling off. Audrey smiled. If she tried to plant her generous bootie on a stool that was already taken, she might hip check some poor jockey into the next county.

As the first of her music selections began to play, she

took a breath and determined to have a good time, even if she danced alone to every song. Since eleven that morning, nasty what-if thoughts had been pelting her brain like buckshot. Sound and movement might drown them out.

Reminding herself that dancing by one's lonesome ranked pretty low on the list of life's injustices, she prepared to dive in—

And then she saw him.

Golden-haired and granite-jawed, over eighteen hands high and as broad as a lumberjack, he seemed bigger than life in every way, as if he'd been carved from the side of a mountain. Earthy, hard-edged and enduring, he gave the startling impression that he had been around since the beginning of time…that he could be around forever.

Since she was a kid, Audrey had been a dedicated people watcher. One of her worst habits, aside from cutting her toenails on the bed, was to file people into categories of her own creation. The stranger at the bar fit neatly into "Blessed At Birth." Born beautiful—and unless she missed her guess, rich—he'd probably developed his taste for designer clothing in preschool.

Despite the dim bar lighting, the man's bloodline was plain as day. He'd been born to win. His suit covered a body clearly trimmed of excess. His hair was perfect, and she'd bet a dollar to a doughnut that his nails were manicured, which made her curl her own fingers into her palm. She was a farrier; she spent more time working on horses' hooves than on her own cuticles.

Audrey didn't date much, but when she did, she had rules. Thoroughbreds were strictly off-limits. All that perfection made her queasy. The men to whom she was attracted were usually local guys from the community college, where she took one class every semester. What the men she dated had in common was that they were not interested in long-term anything (which kept the goodbyes quick and pain-free, exactly how goodbyes should be) and they were average. Not awash in so much testosterone that they seemed like superheroes waiting for a damsel to rescue.

Audrey Griffin was not a girl who believed in knights-in-shining-armor or in being rescued.

Although…

She'd already spent a good dozen of her twenty-four years pulling herself up by her bootstraps. Would it be so awful if she lost herself in a man who looked as if he could vanquish a dragon without breaking a sweat? Just this once.

All day she'd felt as if she were disappearing, bit by tiny bit. The stranger's gaze seemed to bring her back.

And if his gaze is that powerful, imagine what his touch can do.

Heat rushed through her. The man seemed to glow in the darkness of the bar, more beautiful and more mysterious than the others present. Most mysterious of all, he never looked away. Men like him rarely noticed her, and that had never bothered her before, not a bit. Yet…

She couldn't help it; his attention made her feel special, almost…protected.

It was sophomoric; it was foolish. It was the kind of magical thinking she'd abandoned in junior high. Still, she had the feeling that nothing bad could happen if he was with her.

Oh, how she ached to believe the lie for a night.

Her song continued, filling the bar with its intoxicating rhythm.

Throat dry from the whiskey and nerves, Audrey took a step toward the stranger.

And then another.

He continued to watch her, too, and she wished she could better read his expression, but she decided to let the ambiguity be part of the pleasure.

She wasn't a sexy dancer, but she liked to move. Of their own volition, her hips began to sway to the beat. With nerves making her skin tingle, she gave him a smile that she hoped held the invitation to join her on the dance floor. Her mind began to whirl as she reached the place where she had only to raise her voice above the music in order for him to hear her. Should she speak now or wait until she was closer and could whisper the invitation to join her?

Moistening her lipstick-less lips, she drew them back in a smile of invitation, and—

"Kentucky Ale and a Chardonnay." Herman's deep baritone resonated as he placed two glasses in front of Audrey's mystery man. "You want a bowl of peanuts for your table?"

Too quickly, too easily, her fantasy date's attention broke away from her and swung to the bartender. "No, thanks."

Audrey felt the first sickening moments of embarrassment. Two glasses? And one of them a Chardonnay?

He didn't look her way again, not the tiniest glance, as he unrolled bills from a rather thick wad of money, motioned for Herman to keep the change and picked up his drinks. Audrey watched him, trying hard to feel philosophical instead of fourteen, as his smooth gait carried him to a table in the shadowed corner of the bar.

Since his back was to her now, she risked following him with her gaze. Dim lighting or not, the truth was immediately apparent. Waiting for him on the opposite side of the round wood table sat a woman whose beauty seemed otherworldly. Where Audrey was tall with a perfect build for stable work, the other woman looked like a ballerina from the waist-up. A V-neck blouse in soft pink set off her mother-of-pearl skin and delicate collarbones. Audrey wore a short-sleeved, button-down shirt that could have belonged to a man. Her bold auburn hair seemed almost cartoonish compared to the other girl's soft, nut-brown waves. And when the lovely creature smiled, Audrey cringed inside.

She had sent a come-hither smile and wagged her hips at a man whose girlfriend made "perfection" seem like a criminal understatement. She, who had learned long ago that her highly imperfect life made running with the Thoroughbreds of the world about as likely as a draft horse competing in the Derby.

Audrey didn't think she was unattractive. She knew that if she put a little effort into her appearance she could look like…well, a girl. But putting effort into her appearance would defeat her purpose: to weed out imposters.

Life was full of people who had no problem loving you when everything was going right. But throw 'em a

curve—financial ruin, physical hardship, a little ter-
minal illness, say—and the phonies scattered like rats
to a sewer.

Her eyes began to burn. She blinked hard. Lately she
was tired and not above wondering why some lives
seemed to be inherently more graceful, crafted more ex-
quisitely…hell, just plain easier…than others.

Maudlin alert. Stop thinking.

Turning, Audrey let her eyelids drift shut as she
moved to the beat of Cyndi Lauper's quirky vocals,
intent on shutting out every other sound and especially
intent on drowning out her thoughts as she danced alone
toward the middle of the floor.

Raising her arms over her head, she sang along, pretending she believed every word of the lyrics.

"Girls just wanna have fun."

"If your eyebrows dip any lower, you're going to get
hair in your beer."

His tablemate's comment jerked Shane from the odd
trance into which he'd fallen. Reaching for his drink, he
smiled apologetically. "Sorry. I must be jet-lagged."

"Mm-hmm." Hilary Cambria, who'd traveled with
him to Kentucky from their native Australia, and who
looked fresh as a daisy, gave him a pitying look. "You
should be out there, dancing." Pursing the lips Shane
had always thought were one of her best features, she
cocked her head to consider him. "You need to lighten
up, boyo. Live a little." She raised her glass. "Like her."

Shane didn't have to glance over to know whom his
cousin meant. The redhead. The pool shark who bought

shots for her mates and drank whiskey like one of the boys. There'd been so much laughter and melodramatic groaning around the pool table when he and Hilary had first entered the bar, he couldn't help but notice the woman who'd been in the middle of it all.

She behaved as if she hadn't a responsibility in the world. She dressed as if she didn't give a damn, yet she had more men around her than a swimsuit model.

He knew without having to look again that her skin was the color of wheat, her hair a red-brown that was several shades darker than her many freckles. She was tall, strong and curvy like a milk-fed farm girl, her innocent look at odds with her bold personality.

"Live for today, for tomorrow we may die." He'd heard her toast, and frankly it had irritated the hell out of him. He couldn't stomach a cavalier attitude toward life, yet part of him wanted to challenge her to a game of pool and give her a real race for her money. He wanted to spend the night finding out what was truer: the sassy attitude or the fresh-off-the-farm appearance.

Another part of him knew that a woman like the redhead was simply one of life's distractions, and he'd stopped indulging in those years earlier, when he'd realized his need to find a purpose for his life outweighed all other desires.

"I saw you watching her." Hilary interrupted his thoughts. "She wanted to dance with you, you know. She was walking right toward you."

Shane took a sip of his beer, buying himself a moment. He wanted to answer this well.

Returning the frosted glass to a damp cocktail

napkin, he reached across the round table, laying his hand on Hilary's. "I'm with the prettiest girl in the place. And I happen to know she's a great conversationalist. Why would I give all that up for a dance?"

His heart sank when he saw her neat jawline tense.

"Because I'm your cousin. And because dancing… is…fun." She spoke slowly, as if she were addressing a half-wit. "Or don't you like fun anymore?"

Exhaling her anger, she plucked up her wineglass, her blue eyes narrowing above the rim. "You know I love you, but I can't spend all my time babysitting so you won't be lonely. It's starting to put a crimp in my social life."

Understanding her true implication, Shane responded immediately and firmly. "I'm not babysitting you."

"Tell it to someone who hasn't known you since you wore tighty whities."

She took a gulp of wine, and Shane felt the awesome burden of his own ineffectualness. "What, pray tell, are tighty whities?" he asked, mostly to fill time until he figured out how to talk to her. She'd changed so much in the past year.

Surprising him, she laughed, and thankfully the sound wasn't quite as brittle as he might have feared. "You really need to get out more. Tighty whities are men's jocks. The plain kind. Do you know that in America, some men wear jocks that are red-white-and-blue on the Fourth of July? I wonder how they fit all the stars and stripes on there?"

She had decided to make him laugh, and she succeeded. He felt a rush of affection for the girl who had always loved everything American. He hoped this trip to the States would be a gift to her, hoped it would bring back some of her joy.

He was tempted to tease her in return, to lighten the mood still more, but when he looked at her face, he saw that she was already glancing beyond him, her expression so wistful, so rich with longing that he turned to see what was affecting her.

On the dance floor, the redhead had found a partner—a jockey, Shane guessed. Wiry, compact and several inches shorter than the girl, he looked like a dervish, spinning and kicking his seemingly boneless legs out at odd angles. Shane suspected, though, that it was not so much the jockey but the girl whom Hilary watched.

The redhead would never win a dance contest. Like her partner, she flung her arms and legs about in what appeared to be several directions at once. Given her long legs, long neck, plus the russet hair and freckles, he figured he could be forgiven, although probably not by her, for thinking she looked like an enthusiastic giraffe. Once again, his interest caught and held.

When the jockey did a crazy move, kicking one leg way in the air and then spinning around, the woman laughed and matched him move for move.

"She's got the right idea," he heard Hilary murmur with a catch in her voice that made his gut ache. "Dance like there's no tomorrow."

Her eyes swam with pain. She'd never been good at hiding her feelings, even now when, for the first time, she earnestly tried. Immediately Shane felt helpless.

Then he felt the roiling frustration and anger that his helplessness aroused.

"I'm beat," he said, watching her expression. "Mind if we head back to the motel?"

He thought he handled that relatively well, making their hasty retreat about him rather than her, but the twist of her lips said she knew exactly what he was doing, and she snapped.

"Don't coddle me." The rage underlying the low, frustrated growl was so unlike Hilary that even she seemed shocked.

A terrible, impotent grief choked Shane. He wanted to rail at the unfairness of a life that would harm a woman like her, but leave him standing—he, who in thirty-four privileged years had never found a purpose to his existence. Hilary had always been the one with plans, goals. Gratitude. He had been the discontent wanderer.

In a way, he wished Hilary would give him hell, vent her anger on him, say everything that was on her mind, but as swiftly as her anger spiked, it receded. Without another word, she reached for the light wrap draped over the back of her chair. Shane stood, waiting to see whether she would welcome his help or insist on maneuvering herself out of the bar.

As it turned out, she did neither. Allowing her hands to rest limply in her lap, her head bowed forward in an unconscious posture of defeat, she waited silently while he came around behind her and wheeled her back from the table. She neither looked at him nor made a sound as he steered the wheelchair between the bar's narrowly spaced tables.

A year ago, he had been traveling through Central America digging sewers, building an hogar, desperately seeking activities to give his life meaning.

He had meaning now. The same accident that had damaged Hilary's spinal cord had killed her parents, leaving her with sole ownership of Cambria Estates, a vineyard and winery near Sydney, Australia. Shane had returned from Central America immediately—needed. Truly needed for perhaps the first time in his life.

He'd been learning the wine business ever since, set with the task of ensuring that Cambria was strong enough to support Hilary for the rest of her life, if need be.

Standing behind the wheelchair, looking at her beautiful bowed head, he vowed that nothing would throw him off track. He had no interest in "living for today"; not when he had finally found every reason to plan for tomorrow.

Chapter Two

Quest Stables occupied a thousand acres in Woodford County, Kentucky, south of Lexington. It housed five hundred horses, and its stunning size and international reputation often distracted visitors from the land upon which it sat. That was a shame, indeed, because Quest was so exquisite, so resplendently engraved upon the landscape, that it could have been a commercial urging tourists to drop everything and visit the Bluegrass State.

It was true that guests to the stables or to Thomas and Jenna Preston's home often commented on the artistic perfection of the surroundings. If a property could have its colors done, Quest would be a winter—bright and clear and deep. The grass wasn't green; it was emerald. The wildflowers were amethyst and vermilion and bridal-gown white. Copses of oak and pine and aspen softened the strong summer sun, giving the impression that heaven kissed the land with gold.

Still, the pastoral elegance perceived while brunching on the large veranda could be misleading. Behind the veil of gentle living, there thrummed the inevitable activity and workload of an establishment that produced world-class champion racers.

The most recent and most renowned of the Prestons' winners was a bay stallion named Leopold's Legacy. Two months earlier, the handsome brute had won the Derby, followed by a dazzling victory at the Preakness that suggested more wins and high stud fees in his future. He was what every owner and trainer hungered for—a horse that could become a legend.

But Legacy's ride to the top had been marred. A routine DNA test proved that his sire was not the champion Apollo's Ice, as originally recorded, and the Prestons, who so recently had stood in the winner's circle, now found themselves in the middle of a breeding scandal. The reputation and financial future of the entire organization were in danger.

Most mornings for the past month, Quest's difficulties had been the first thing on Audrey's mind. She awoke worrying about Brent Preston, Quest's breeder, and about Carter Phillips, their veterinarian. More than anyone, the two men were coming under suspicion from the Jockey Association. Only Thoroughbreds produced by live cover rather than artificial insemination were accepted for the association's registration, and both Brent and Carter had witnessed the breeding of

Leopold's Legacy's dam, Courtin' Cristy, with Apollo's Ice at Angelina's Stud Farm.

Audrey knew the Prestons well and trusted them implicitly. They had been beyond reproach as employers to both her father, who had served as their head farrier for eleven years, and her since she took his place last year. Shoeing Thoroughbreds was the only work she had ever known. Her father had been her hero and best friend, and she'd trailed him like a puppy through the stables while he worked. Treating her like one of the team instead of a youthful nuisance, the Prestons had made it easy for her to follow in her dad's footsteps.

Feeling impotent in the face of their current troubles, she had readily agreed to help by pulling names up from Quest's database so the Prestons could contact the owners of their stabled horses. The family wanted to personally break the news that the Jockey Association had recalled Leopold's Legacy's Thoroughbred status, which meant the regional racing commissions refused to let him race in North America. Several owners already had withdrawn horses stabled at Quest after the first whiff of scandal, and the Prestons were hoping to stanch further losses by reaching their clients before industry gossip did.

Printing phone lists didn't feel very proactive, but it was better than sitting on one's hands, and if it helped Brent and Carter even a little bit, then it was worth it.

Rolling over in bed the morning after she'd danced the night away, Audrey realized this was the first time in weeks that she'd awoken to find her thoughts consumed by her own circumstances as much as by the Prestons'.

Bending an arm above her head, she gazed at the ceiling, recently painted a crisp white, and tried to guess the time without looking at the clock. It was a workday, and she almost always rose before five on a workday, but the brightness and warmth in the room suggested she'd overslept.

Of course, the warmth could be attributed to the big body in bed next to her. A faint disgust had her shaking her head. She'd been exhausted when her head hit the pillow, but she was reasonably certain she'd climbed into bed alone.

"How did you get in here?" she asked without looking over, wrinkling her nose at the answer—a rude snort in her ear.

"Seamus," she scolded, rolling toward a hundred-and-sixty pounds of lean muscle, wiry steel-gray hair and huge feet. Four of them. "You're supposed to be sleeping at the big house. Thomas and Jenna bought you that beautiful bed. Don't be an ingrate."

The mammoth Irish wolfhound responded by swiping a sleepy tongue over Audrey's face then yawning. Hugely.

"Morning breath, Seamus."

Audrey sat up. Her bedroom window, which she'd left open, was once again missing its screen, pried off by the one male on the property that had fallen hopelessly, madly in love with her.

Leaving Seamus where he was—not a morning man, he'd be snoring before her feet hit the floor—Audrey hauled herself out of bed and slogged toward the living area of her small home, one of the employee cottages on the Prestons' estate.

She'd have liked to have started her day straight off with a mug of painfully strong coffee, but she'd ignored a blinking light on her phone machine the night before. Prioritizing, she padded down her short hallway and pressed "play" on the machine that sat on the maple-topped bar dividing her kitchen and living room.

"Audrey," the first message began, *"Carter here. Melanie spotted a problem with Something to Talk About's gait a couple of days ago. I haven't found a cause, but I noticed he's due for a shoeing, so can you give me a call when you get around to him? Thanks."* Beep.

Making a mental note, Audrey went to the fridge and withdrew a pound bag of ground coffee beans. She grabbed a filter and a measuring spoon so she could start her eight-cup-a-day habit as the next message played. She was so freakishly tired from yesterday, she thought she might up the ante to ten cups.

"Hi, Audrey." Halting with the measuring spoon in the coffee bag, Audrey turned her head toward the machine. The voice alone made her feel cold all over. *"It's Dr. McFarland. I don't have the results of your blood tests yet, obviously, but when you left my office today, I got the sense you might not follow up with the surgeon I recommended. So I'm calling because…"*

Dr. McFarland paused, and Audrey found herself hoping that the internist had mistakenly hung up or been cut off. No such luck.

"Audrey, I've known you a long time, and I understand how difficult it would be if you were sick again, but I—"

Lunging for the phone machine, Audrey pressed "skip."

Heart beating as if she'd already injected caffeine

into a major artery, she set her jaw and breathed deeply through her nose.

No, you don't understand.

"I'm not sick again." Breathe in, two-three-four… *I am not sick.* Breathe out, two-three…

The next message had already begun, and Audrey made herself concentrate on Jenna Preston's upbeat voice, hoping it would calm the buzzing in her brain.

"…calling to invite you to lunch tomorrow. I hope you can make it. You don't have to call back, honey. Just come on up to the house at noon. See you tomorrow unless I bump into you before. Bye."

When the phone machine clicked off, Audrey closed her eyes and stood very still.

A year ago, her dad had died unexpectedly of a heart attack at the age of sixty-four. Henry Griffin had been her only relative, her roommate, her rock. Since his passing, Jenna's kindness had swelled into a motherly concern that made Audrey feel guilty, because she knew in her heart that it was time for her to leave Quest. The call from Dr. McFarland confirmed the instinct.

She and her dad had moved here from Texas when Audrey was twelve. Certainly it had occurred to her in recent years that a twenty-something ought to experience more of the world than a piece of Kentucky, but until her father's passing, she had never seriously entertained the idea of leaving. She figured that was why she took so many dang classes—so she could be an armchair adventurer. But now that he was gone, was it enough? She had a little money; she could travel, see places she'd only read about. She was twenty-four, and she'd never been in an airplane.

Opening her eyes and abandoning the coffee, she crossed slowly to the living room, to a recliner that sat just inside the front door. Neatly positioned beside the chair, rested a pair of burgundy-green-and-navy plaid men's slippers made soft and pliable from lots of wear.

As if the slippers belonged to her, Audrey slid her feet inside. Her stress melted into the faux sheepskin lining. She'd given Henry the loafers as a joke Christmas gift one year—slippers that matched his favorite plaid chair. He'd worn them every night after work, claiming, "My big ol' feet never looked better." Memories rose from the shoes' very soles… The way her dad laughed like a cartoon chipmunk: *"Chee-chee-chee-chee."* The Sunday morning going-to-church scent of Aqua Velva aftershave. The soft expression in his eyes when she sometimes caught him watching her.

"God must think I'm an okay sort, Audrey Lea, because He gave me an angel to love."

Audrey shook her head. She was no angel. Angels didn't get so scared piss-less that they wanted to crawl under their beds and stay there.

She'd always known her future was a big question mark. She'd never had the luxury of taking it for granted, as other people her age were privileged to do.

What she did have was an appreciation for the fragility of life. She needed to carpe diem while there was still a diem to carpe.

Seamus's toenails clicked slowly down the hallway as the big lug made his way sleepily toward the living room.

"Decided you couldn't live without me, huh?"

Meeting him halfway, Audrey leaned over for a sloppy kiss and a wirehaired hug. The problem with saying hello to a new life was the necessity of bidding goodbye to the old one first.

"I love you, you big goof, but it's time for you to find a girl your own age. Preferably your own species." When she straightened, he whined. "Come on, I'll make breakfast and show you some of the travel brochures I've been collecting."

As they walked to the kitchen, Audrey considered the past year of breakfasts shared only with her four-footed friend. Then she remembered the brief moment of excitement and anticipation in the bar last night.

"To tell you the truth, Seamus, I wouldn't mind waking up next to someone my own species, too. It wouldn't be anything serious, so don't get your whiskers in a knot. But I'm thinking I could combine travel with a little romance. I hear Frenchmen are a lot of fun. And they know how to let go when the time comes."

"Shove over, you big, beautiful nag."

Leaning her shoulder heavily into a shining gray filly named Biding Her Time, Audrey waited for the horse to shift her weight. Biding leaned the opposite way, forcing Audrey to drop the filly's hoof and stand up—or be squashed by several hundred pounds of Thoroughbred.

"Sheesh!" Pulling her gloves off her hands, she slapped them to the ground. "You are the most stubborn damn thing."

Showing more initiative than he ordinarily did during

daylight hours, Seamus bounded off a comfortable bed of hay in one of Quest's many stables and came to Audrey's defense, growling at the horse.

Biding gave him the evil eye, stamped her hoof and whinnied. Untied, she wouldn't be above trying to knock the dog down.

"Better leave her alone, Seamus, you know how cranky she gets. Besides, this is my job."

Audrey had played or worked around horses all her life, and truthfully she liked the crafty and opinionated beasts best. Biding Her Time was one of those. After several races in which she had yet to place, a number of people were prepared to write her off. Not Audrey. She knew, or sensed anyway, that the filly was testing the waters, not merely in races, but in her life. Biding paid attention to everything in the stable, in the paddock, on the track. She investigated her surroundings as if she were waiting for the *click* that would inspire her to think, *I'm home, I'm safe, I'm ready to win.*

Pushing back the locks of hair that had fallen loose from her braid and plucking at the T-shirt that glommed ickily to her damp skin, Audrey went forehead to forehead with the filly. "I certainly hope you're ready to get new shoes, 'cause they're coming, whether you like it or not."

Repositioning herself, Audrey picked up the left front hoof, quickly shoving her shoulder under the horse. Biding relented, allowing her foot to be placed between Audrey's bent knees and the pedicure to begin. It was a game they had played for the past year. They both enjoyed it.

"Atta girl." Audrey began filing and soon was immersed in the sound of the hoof being grated down, the "Classic Strings" CD on the player perched atop a stool a few feet away, and the huff-huff-huff of Biding's breathing.

This was the part of the job Audrey liked best—the soothing rhythm, the juxtaposition of quiet solitude and labor that was hard enough to soak her hairline, chest and back with perspiration. She'd have to finish her morning work in time for a shower before lunch. Which was a real waste of personal grooming, if you asked her, because she had two more ponies to shoe that afternoon.

The sad truth was that she'd rather plant herself on a chair outside Biding's stall, chow down on a turkey-and-Swiss on rye and sneak the horse a few carrots, than join the Prestons at the big house. She knew today would present an ideal opportunity to tell the Prestons they needed to hire a new farrier, and she could feel her stomach churning at the prospect.

Turning toward the backpack she usually lugged with her to the stables, Audrey withdrew a roll of the antacids she'd been wolfing down lately. Peeling back the silver paper, she tilted her head, popped two tablets into her mouth and began to chew, quickly deciding this was going to be at least a three-antacid morning.

"Audrey Griffin, don't you dare fill up on candy before lunch. We are having a veritable feast, and I expect you to arrive hungry!"

Startled by her employer's voice, Audrey nearly choked on the tablets.

She whipped around. "Jenna!" Immediately upon seeing the woman's genteel, humor-filled face, she felt tension wring her intestines like a wet towel. "I didn't hear you come up. I…I guess I was busy thinking…I have to finish shoeing Biding, and it's getting pretty close to noon already, so maybe…"

The lame attempt she was about to make to wriggle out of lunch died on her lips when she realized that Jenna had a companion.

"Audrey, dear, I'd like you to meet Shane Preston, our nephew. He's here from Australia. We decided to take a quick tour of the stables before lunch."

Audrey blinked, as if that could change the scene in front of her. Raising the back of her wrist to her forehead, she wiped away a sheen of perspiration that now was due to more than physical exertion.

"Shane, this lovely girl is Audrey Griffin. You'll get to know each other better later, of course."

His brows spiked over the word "lovely." Audrey saw it and was torn between wanting to run home to change her clothes and the desire to chuck a horseshoe at his head.

"Good to meet you, Audrey." Dressed in a pristine suit on a scorching Kentucky day, the man smiled with just a quirk of his lips. His smooth Australian accent underscored the sardonic expression.

So the stranger in the bar, the one who looked as if he belonged on Mt. Rushmore or some other wonder of the world, was a Preston. It figured.

Handsome and strong like the Thoroughbreds they raised, the Prestons possessed physical gifts in extra measure. Melanie, a jockey, was a tiny thing, but she sparkled like a diamond and seemed as durable. The

Preston men were all life-size Ken dolls—rock solid, absurdly handsome and short on chatter.

Aussie Ken was no exception.

"Nice to meet you, too." Audrey ducked her sweaty head, hoping he did not recognize her as the girl who had made goo-goo eyes at him last night. And then she realized he was holding out his hand.

She stuck hers out, too, a reflex reaction that she lamented when they touched callus to callus. His palm was much tougher than she had imagined.

Unfortunately, he looked surprised, too. He'd taken her hand gently; she'd automatically used her customary grip, practically squeezing the life out of him.

She meant to let go immediately, but for the briefest of moments, the stable that was the center of her life faded away; the snuffling of horses and mucking of stalls, the scents of hay and manure; horses and humans were replaced by a blanket-like silence.

She realized she was staring, her palm locked with his. Last night's curiosity about his eyes was satisfied: they were the intense blue of marbles and morning skies.

As her heart beat painfully in her throat, Audrey remembered her comment to Seamus—that she was going to find someone of her own species.

Recalling his beautiful companion from the night before, she told herself the truth: *This man is not your species. He looks better, he smells better, and he keeps better company.*

When she noted the humor in his gaze, she let go of his hand as if it had burst into flame. Setting her jaw, Audrey gave him a tough, take-no-prisoners glare.

From the age of nine until well into her teens, she'd been sick and skinny and deathly pale beneath her freckles. In her experience, people reacted to sick children by coddling or pitying or pretending not to notice them. Most of the time, she'd felt out of step with her peers, so she'd trailed her dad around the stables and got to know horses better than people. She'd also learned to act a lot tougher than she was, turning into a real snot when she sensed disapproval or condescension.

So now she embraced the dirt and the calluses and the perspiration, her styleless clothing and the lack of makeup, and sent her gaze on a lazy trip down his body and back up again. Sniffing as if *he* was the one who smelled bad, she drawled, "You sure are dressed pretty for a stroll through a stable. Hope you got the memo about watching where you step."

Good teeth showed in a calculating smile. "I stand forewarned. And thank you for the compliment." He inclined his head. "I have a great admiration, too, for people like you who put so much care into their... *horses'* grooming." He'd paused just long enough to make his inference crystal clear.

Clear to Audrey, at any rate. Jenna didn't seem to notice. Before Audrey could think of a comeback, Jenna said, "Audrey has a natural touch with horses. She's an excellent farrier."

Aussie Ken's brows rose. Either he was surprised or doubtful, or he didn't know what a farrier was. She chose the last interpretation just for the fun of it.

"That means I shoe the nice ponies." She offered the explanation kindly, as if she were talking to a toddler.

She managed to curl the edges of his smile. "I'm familiar with the term."

A calculating light gleamed behind the blue eyes, and Audrey felt her anticipation spike as she wondered whether he'd give her a decent run for her money.

"It's an interesting occupation for a—" Once more he paused, this time furrowing his brow as if he couldn't quite find the right word. "—woman."

Dang!

Round One to Aussie Ken.

"I think we'll let you get on with your work now, Audrey." Becoming aware of the crackle between her nephew and her employee, but not at all sure what to make of it, Jenna verbally stepped between them. "You two can get to know each other better at lunch. Twelve o'clock sharp."

Taking Shane's arm and giving Audrey a bemused look over her shoulder, Jenna guided her nephew on through the stable.

Short of a natural disaster, it looked as if she was having lunch with the Prestons and their nephew. Audrey expected her stomach to clench, but felt it growl instead. Bantering with him must have burned up a few calories.

Absently patting Biding's neck, Audrey chewed her lip. Over the years, she had carved out a place for herself among the largely male population of Quest by learning to compete. At pool, at darts, with words—she gave as good as she got. Often better.

She felt a fluttering in her blood that made her feel more alive than she had all year. What harm could come from trading a few quips? Putting the pretty boy in his place? Shane Preston was a challenge, and her life up to this point had pretty much addicted her to a dare.

A grin stretched across her lips. Picking up her tools, Audrey gave the gray filly a pat on her rump. "Okay, Biding, let's get this shoe on the road. It seems I've worked up quite an appetite."

Chapter Three

Audrey was showered and dressed in a fresh pair of jeans when she lifted the brass doorknocker that reminded her of a ring through a bull's nose. She'd plaited her hair in a French braid this time—simple enough as it hung down her back, but a nod to the fact that she was dining somewhere more upscale than the inside of a stall.

Audrey smiled as the Prestons' housekeeper answered the door and directed her to the patio that lay beyond the elegant white French doors off the dining room.

She had brought Seamus with her, and he followed her as far as the dining room, which was set with a stunning array of white-on-white china, and crystal that gleamed in the sun-kissed room. A polished cherrywood coffee trolley was already set with two glossy silver pots plus a four-tier dessert tree presenting an assortment of miniature cakes and truffles. Everything in the Prestons' home bespoke of a lifestyle made luxurious by financial success.

What would happen to a family used to the finer things in life, if their current troubles proved powerful enough to crumple what they'd built?

There were people, certainly, who would be glad to watch a successful racing family lose at something. Even within the organization, there were always one or two dissenters intent on resenting the very people who signed their paychecks, but Audrey would never be one of them. She admired the Prestons. They worked hard, and at least one of them—Robbie, the youngest son—played hard, but you'd never see them throwing around their money or their power; they simply weren't that way.

On top of that, they'd been good to her. Shortly after she and her dad had moved in—a single father and a skinny, morose-looking preteen who had recently lost her mother and most of her trust in the world—then eighteen-year-old Melanie Preston had arrived with a basket of food and books for Audrey that would have made any welcoming committee feel miserly by comparison. Quickly following his sister's visit, sixteen-year-old Robbie had stopped by to see if any necessary repairs had been noted around the cottage.

When Audrey was sick and stayed home from school for weeks on end, the impromptu visits and special care packages continued and no one had ever made her feel like an extra appendage around the place, even when she surely had been one.

Standing now at the entrance to the dining room, with Seamus sniffing longingly in the direction of the coffee trolley, Audrey hoped that the ambiguity surrounding the breeding of Leopold's Legacy would soon be resolved, preferably before she left the Prestons.

She ruffled the fur around Seamus's neck. "Go find your bed, boy, and have a little nap."

Sadly aware that the dining room was off-limits, the wolfhound turned and trudged off toward the family room where his bed awaited him.

Audrey moved toward the French doors, their glass panes veiled by sheer white curtain panels that allowed in a dreamy, filtered light.

Turning one brass door handle, she let herself out to a wide brick patio dotted with umbrellas that provided big circles of welcoming shade.

Despite a discomfiting hitch of nervousness, Audrey thought she'd managed to walk onto the patio as if she fit in fine with her surroundings.

Jenna and Shane stood by the patio balustrade, listening to Brent Preston, eldest son and head trainer at the stables, while the three of them looked out onto one of the paddocks. Brent's sister, Melanie, and their father, Thomas, were having an animated discussion next to the hors d'oeuvres. Melanie had a glass of iced tea in one hand and a mini ham-and-cheese biscuit in the other. She waved the biscuit when she saw Audrey.

"Come here. I'm telling Dad about Something to Talk About. Audrey, isn't he a beaut? Have you noticed his expression right before he gallops? He's the most naturally ambitious horse I've ever seen. And he tunes in so well to people. He's a total flirt. I bet he'll win just to show off for me."

Thomas watched his daughter with a heartwarming blend of affection and consternation. Horses had been in his blood before they'd ever become his livelihood. He'd lived and breathed racing long before his children had been a glimmer in his eye. He was an old-time track man, however, and the idea that a racehorse of any worth would win or lose depending on his *affection* for a jockey was pushing the boundaries of his belief system. There were still plenty of people, Audrey knew, who did not subscribe to the notion that horses possessed anything approaching emotional intelligence.

She, on the other hand, liked the idea. Working with horses day in and day out gave her a clear impression of which animals had compassion, empathy and a sense of camaraderie, and which wouldn't let you on their backs if you were stranded in a desert without any shoes of your own.

Audrey thought Melanie could be one of the great jockeys someday and smiled as the petite firecracker turned to her now, an anxious frown working between her brows. "You don't think Something's toes are too short, do you, Audrey? His stride seems a little shorter than usual, and I know you don't like long toes, but I'm just wondering… No offense."

"You're not offending me."

As far as Audrey could tell, every shoer did some things his or her own way. Leaving a horse's toes a bit long to lengthen its stride was the tradition at many racetracks, but Audrey's father hadn't believed in it, and neither did she.

Melanie had taken a particular shine to Something to Talk About, so was naturally a bit more…focused…on all the details of his care and training.

Gently, but with authority, Audrey reminded the other woman, "Studies have never shown that long toes lengthen the stride. Just the opposite. Thanks to videos, it's a proven fact that they don't." It was also a fact that plenty of track farriers and even more owners still held on to the mistaken belief, so she added, "Even if it were true, some horses just can't handle a long toe, and I'd never risk the leg to lengthen the stride."

It was a bold thing to state in front of a racing stable's owner—that you wouldn't sacrifice safety to help create a winner—and Thomas wasn't the only one who gave her his full attention.

Both Brent and Shane turned to consider her, Brent mirroring his father's approval, Shane shooting her a keen stare lined by curiosity.

She concentrated her response on Melanie. "I watched Something to Talk About in the paddock this morning, and I think it may be worth an X-ray to see if he's a bit flat-footed. That could change the way I file him."

Melanie was pacified enough to offer Audrey one of the petite ham-and-cheese sandwiches. Hungry, Audrey felt her mouth water as her fingertips closed on the flaky golden biscuit, but it turned gummy on her tongue when Shane excused himself from Jenna and Brent and headed her way.

She felt both relieved and acutely disappointed when he stopped beside Thomas and struck up a conversation about the frustration of participating in claiming stakes, in which horses could be purchased prior to the race and therefore forfeited by the owner regardless of the race's outcome.

Audrey wanted to listen. Rather annoyingly, she caught herself wanting to listen to every word Shane Preston said. Contrary to her earlier assumption, the gorgeous brunette was nowhere in sight. When Jenna announced that it was time to proceed to the dining room, no one mentioned waiting for Shane's girlfriend.

"This is my exit cue," Brent said, giving his mother a peck on the cheek and apologizing to his cousin for missing lunch. "The girls only have a half day at summer camp today, so we're going on a picnic."

"Bring the girls by later," Jenna offered. "I'll take 'em swimming."

Brent agreed and headed out to his own life, which, no matter the complexities of Quest business, centered on the needs of his twin daughters.

Ushering the remaining Prestons plus Audrey to the dining room, Jenna directed Shane to the chair on Audrey's left. Looking at the lovely table and linens and the raw silk cushions adorning each straight-backed chair, Audrey wished that she'd been less committed to individualism when she'd dressed for lunch and more concerned with being appropriate. Even Melanie, who typically dressed as if she were ready for a workout, had donned a casual summer dress.

Before she could dwell on it, Shane surprised her by

pulling out her chair. Mumbling her thank-you, Audrey reached for the chair to scoot herself in, nearly cannoning into the table before she realized that Shane was smoothly sliding the chair in for her.

Her plan to continue their verbal swordplay at lunch seemed overly ambitious now. One whiff of Shane's light cologne tangled her thoughts.

Geez, Audrey, he's just a guy.

"How old are Brent's daughters?" Shane asked as he took his own seat.

"Eight." Thomas boomed the answer like a proud grandfather, earning a look of affection from his wife. "My favorite age."

"Hey, you told me thirty-one was your favorite age." Melanie needled, her eyes laughing at her father. "Dad pretends I'm still his favorite," she said to Shane and Audrey, "but you can't compete with grandchildren."

Thomas and Jenna both demurred, but abashedly. "The twins have needed more attention since their mother's passing," Jenna admitted with a sigh. "I think sometimes we're guilty of spoiling them."

"We were all sorry to hear about Brent's wife. I know my mother wished she could help. Being so far away, it was hard to know what to do."

Shane's deep, accented voice fell on the room like cotton, soft but substantial, changing the mood. Audrey saw Jenna and Melanie glance immediately to Thomas and sensed that Shane had just apologized for something more than not knowing what to do when Brent's wife died.

Audrey had heard through the Quest grapevine that Thomas and his brother David had been estranged for years. One brother made his mark on horse racing in the United States; the other had staked his claim thousands of miles away in Australia, operating a horseracing stable there. Recently the frayed edges of the family had been knitted together when Thomas and Jenna attended some huge shindig in Australia. Knowing Jenna, Audrey figured Shane had been heartily invited to Quest.

"Nothing to do," Thomas answered his nephew gruffly. "Even if things had been different between me and your father, there wasn't anything anyone could do to make losing our daughter-in-law easier on Brent or the girls."

Shane inclined his head respectfully. Audrey thought his careful inspection of Thomas was quite telling. He addressed his uncle deferentially, watching him closely, and yet she knew with a certainty that surprised her that Shane Preston did not defer to many people. Perhaps he was here on a peacemaking mission for his branch of the family?

Drawing circles in the moisture on her water goblet, she waited uncomfortably as the silence extended. Jenna seemed unusually quiet and contemplative; Thomas's lower lip jutted out as he broke the Parker House roll on his bread plate; Melanie was clearly thinking about something that had nothing to do with anyone at the table; and Shane…

She angled her head to take a look at him. Still concentrating on Thomas, he felt Audrey's gaze and turned slowly. Raising one thick brow the color of honey, he managed to look both challenging and amused without moving a single other part of his face.

Somehow she didn't feel embarrassed for being caught staring. She knew he was off-limits, but that didn't stop the heat that twined through her veins. Curiously, she took stock of her feelings.

Excited? Check.

Feeling daring? Check.

Physically aroused? That would be a double check.

At twenty-four, she had slept with two men, which placed her far behind her peers in terms of practical experience, to say nothing of the fact that she had never been in love. She'd had a terrifyingly large crush once on Robbie Preston, the youngest and most breathtakingly reckless of Thomas and Jenna's four offspring, but that had gone the way of other youthful fantasies.

Shane resembled the two men who had been her lovers…not in the slightest, actually. They'd been studious, sweet, tame. So had the sex, though she had only her own imagination and a couple of books for comparison. But it had seemed tame. Memorable mostly for its newness.

As the meal was served, Shane turned his head to answer some question that Jenna raised, and Audrey studied his profile.

Recalling his presence in the bar, how he had stood out from the others, she doubted any woman would ever call him tame. If last night had turned out differently—if he hadn't been with another woman, but instead had shown a serious interest in her—would she have ditched caution and made a dive for excitement?

She stared at his hands—large and strong with clean nails—as he reached for a water goblet and she had a sudden image of those big, experienced, untamed hands on her breasts.

Beneath the confines of a rather sturdy cotton bra, her nipples tightened.

For Pete's sake.

Transferring her gaze to the salt and pepper shakers, she tried to distract her body. But the question persisted: had the opportunity presented itself, would she have seized the moment? One incredibly sexy, lusty moment the likes of which she'd never before experienced and might never again?

Would you, Audrey?

I don't know.

Would you?

I—don't—know.

Would you?

"Would you?"

"Yes! Yes!" In the silence that met her exclamation, Audrey glanced around the table. *Uh-oh.*

Fairly certain that last "Would you?" had emanated from somewhere other than her own thoughts, she looked up to see Eva Franklin, the Prestons' brilliant cook, standing beside her. In a much smaller voice, Audrey said, "Could you repeat the question?"

"Would you like mango hollandaise, Miss Audrey?" Poor Eva looked uncertain, poised to ladle a thick peach-colored sauce atop the plate of salmon Audrey hadn't even noticed being set in front of her. The deep spoon of sauce hovered precariously between gravy boat and plate.

Smiling brilliantly at the kind, middle-aged woman,

Audrey tried to cover her tracks by nodding enthusiastically. "Yes! Yes! I would!"

Eva smiled back and covered the fish in a thick film of mango hollandaise. Melanie regarded Audrey quizzically from across the table, while beside her, Shane smirked.

As Eva moved on around the table, Shane inquired in a wiseass undertone, "Are you a fan of all tropical fruits, Miss Griffin, or is the mango a particular favorite?"

His smile mocked her. She had the incredibly disturbing sensation that he knew exactly what she'd been thinking.

Picking up her fork, she took a poke at her salmon. "I try not to discriminate against produce."

"Commendable. I'm a staunch supporter of the kiwi myself. Try to attend all the rallies, go door-to-door for the cause when necessary."

Such a wiseass.

"That sounds time-consuming. What do you do for a living? No! Don't tell me. I'll guess."

Giving him a good long look, as if he wasn't already an indelible imprint on her brain, she ventured, "You're an…undertaker."

Jenna gasped. Thomas and Melanie laughed, and the man in question spit up a little bit of ice water.

The look he gave her—surprised, amused, a little irritated—sent a buzz of excitement running through her body and pooling low, low in her belly.

"What tipped you off?" he said, dabbing his lips with the napkin—the perfect gentleman, though his voice was low and laced with challenge.

In that moment, he reminded her of a tiger pretending to be full while a gazelle strolled by. No matter how relaxed he looked, he could pounce when least expected.

Unfortunately, she couldn't convince herself to change her course.

Reaching for the roll on her bread plate, Audrey broke a piece off, popped it into her mouth and spoke around it. "The dark suits, I suppose. And the fact that you have a stick up your—"

Pausing while she faked a need to concentrate on her chewing, she swallowed and completed her sentence.

"—back." Then she widened her eyes and tried to look innocent. "You have really good posture."

Chapter Four

So she wanted to wrangle.

Shane came close to giving in to the temptation to cross swords with the idiosyncratic woman beside him.

Carefully avoiding eye contact with the others around the table, he slid his fork into his salmon and considered his various strong reactions to Audrey Griffin.

Even now that she was cleaned up, she looked no more formal than she had in the bar. Jeans that were designed to be serviceable rather than sexy appeared to be her uniform, a damned disappointment given the obvious shapeliness of the body beneath them. Her freckled skin was toasted to an appealing tan by the sun, and her hair, still damp from a shower, was the color of wet bricks. The lack of makeup and the plain rubber band holding her long braid made him think of a hard-working pioneer woman.

The disparity between her appearance and her personality did not escape him. A first glance at Audrey Griffin suggested someone guileless and straightforward, perhaps philosophical, definitely sweet. Then she opened her mouth and all he could think was trouble.

He was thirty-four, thank God, not twenty. Several years ago, he may have gotten to know her better for her audacity alone. Now he had a business and a life to build. A reckless young woman out for a good time was not on his radar.

"Thank you for the compliment, Miss Griffin," he said with boring neutrality. "I look forward to telling my parents that their insistence on cotillion classes did not go to waste."

"Did you really take cotillion?" Melanie eyed him with suspicion. "Mom tried to coerce us, but Brent and Robbie threatened to run away from home. I went twice and both times the instructor ended the class with a horrible migraine. She'd never had one before, so it was agreed all around that I could quit." She shifted her gaze. "Audrey, did your dad ever send you to cotillion or did you escape that nightmare?"

Audrey hesitated. Lines of tension formed around her lips before she visibly forced herself to smile. "I escaped."

She ducked her head, and Shane was certain that she blushed. Curiosity mingled with sympathy, because it was pretty damned obvious that the audacious young woman had never taken a course on manners or conventional grace.

Then Shane realized what Melanie had revealed: Audrey had had a father, but no mother. It might be the mention of that fact or something else, but Audrey was suddenly acutely uncomfortable.

While Melanie and her parents debated the merits of cotillion, he reached spontaneously for Audrey's hand and gave it a sympathetic squeeze. To his surprise, she jumped as if he'd stuck her with his fork. Her blush deepened, flushing not only her cheeks, but also her chest and even a few splotchy areas on her arms. Fidgeting, she reached up to tuck her hair behind her ear, unnecessary as it was already scraped back into a braid, but the movement drew his attention to the scar on her neck.

Standing out white against her reddened skin, the scar ran from behind her ear to below the collar of her shirt.

"We're pouring one of your wines, Shane." Thomas commanded his attention, raising a bottle of Chardonnay that had been uncorked in the kitchen. "We're not as sophisticated about this as I'm sure you are. I'm a Kentucky bourbon man. So if there's something special you want us to—"

"I'd be happy to act as your sommelier, if you'll allow me." Shane rose, awaiting permission to take the bottle from his uncle.

"Sommelier, huh?" Thomas huffed, half impressed and half gently mocking. "Around here we call that bartending." He held out the bottle. "Have at it."

Adrenaline pulsed through Shane as he rounded the table and accepted the wine.

This was why he was in the U.S. This bottle in his hands was his future. Hilary's future.

Respectfully, he poured an inch of Chardonnay into Thomas's wineglass and another inch into Jenna's. He didn't believe in gender bias when it came to choosing a good wine. And he knew his aunt was more likely to be of service to him and to Hilary on this business trip.

He watched her expression, especially, as she swirled the glass briefly and took her first sip.

Her brow furrowed just a bit, perhaps due to the fear she might not like his product. But then she relaxed and smiled. "Delicious. I'm not a connoisseur, but I'd order it in a restaurant. It has the most interesting combination of fruit and…I'm not sure…herbs?" She tasted again. "I'll remember it."

I'll remember it.

Those three words were like music to Shane. He endeavored to appear relaxed and connected, despite the excitement coursing through him.

For years he'd bounced from job to job, trying to excavate some meaning out of each one. When he dug and came up empty-handed, he moved on, his hunt for purpose and passion nearly desperate. Throughout his twenties, he had responded to each dashed hope by distracting himself for a time—with women, with a broken-down boat he'd sailed from Perth to Maui, with a trek through Central America carrying nothing but a backpack and a map.

In his adolescence, he'd watched his parents and even his younger brother slot into exactly what made life worth living for them. He'd taken for granted that he would find his own reason for being, but that sense of rightness had eluded him.

There had been times when he'd wondered whether his search had been so much harder because he had craved meaning. He remembered feeling a restless hunger even when he was a kid—wanting every walk he took to leave a footprint.

He'd still been searching last year when Hilary's accident brought him home to Australia. He hadn't expected to find his groove running the winery that had belonged to her parents, but that's what was happening.

Lochlain, the family's stable, adjoined Cambria Estates Vineyard. As a boy, he'd spent almost as much time among the grapevines as he had at Lochlain. He'd worked at Cambria on school vacations when his father had granted permission not to work at the stable, but he'd never considered a career as a vintner.

He'd arrived in Hunter Valley last year, committed only to doing what he could for his cousin. He hadn't cared that he was growing grapes. He'd have grown damned zinnias if it would have helped. But one morning, months after he'd arrived, he'd awoken thinking about grapes, smelling them, curious about every aspect of the winery. Not long after, he'd realized that—for the first time in his life—he wasn't thinking about where to go next. Feet on the earth, hands on the vines, mind wrapped around the art and science of being a vintner, he'd found something with a history and a future. He could plant more than grapes; he could plant the seeds of his life, and they would grow into a legacy.

He planned to attend a series of wine shows in New York, Boston and Montreal, introducing his product to the international market. By the time he and Hilary returned to Australia, Cambria Estates would be the wine that people were talking about.

There was only one problem he could foresee: although he'd learned much about wine, he didn't know a damned thing about wine shows.

By the time he'd filled each glass and resumed his seat at the table, his elevated mood had dropped a bit.

Beside him, Audrey was picking apart her salmon, lost in thoughts of her own and seeming to have forgotten her earlier desire to spar. Across the table, his cousin Melanie was happily engaged in a discourse with her father and anyone else who cared to join in. The topic, of course: horses and racing. Thomas listened avidly to his daughter while simultaneously scowling at his fish, as though he would trade his best dirt runner for a decent burger.

Shane wasn't sure what he'd expected to achieve today; he knew only that he felt as if he were in a starting gate, about to race for his life and now facing an agonizingly long wait for the bell.

He stuck the tines of his fork into a piece of grilled asparagus, picked up his knife and told himself to be a good guest, that everything would happen in due time. He didn't have long to wait.

"I don't think your question about Shane's occupation was ever properly answered, was it, Audrey?"

With a hint of good humor, Jenna pulled Audrey out of her reverie. The confounding redhead looked up and shook her head. "He's not an undertaker?" she muttered.

Jenna arched a brow that made Audrey obediently apply herself to her meal as her employer continued. "This delicious wine we're drinking is a sample of

Shane's work. He's here to introduce his vineyard to the United States."

Not exactly "his" vineyard—Cambria was owned by Hilary and her grandparents—but he supposed that was close enough under the circumstances. They had offered to make him a full partner.

"Shane will be attending several wine exhibits," Jenna told the table at large. "What you don't know is that he asked me to help him find an assistant to work in his booth. Wine exhibits require a minimum of two people per booth." She pulsed with energy as she smiled at her audience. "I've been doing my research. One person to serve and one to answer questions and keep track of the guest book. A sole proprietor at the booth also detracts from the cache of the winery. I know it's terribly superficial, but appearances really do count. It would have been difficult for Shane to interview and hire the perfect person all the way from Australia, which is why—" she raised her glass, the wine glowing from the lights of the crystal chandelier above their heads and the sunlight filtering through the curtained doors "—I've arranged everything. I think it's best to have one assistant at all times, in New York, Boston and Montreal. The same assistant for the sake of continuity, and won't it be pleasant to have a traveling companion? I love to travel with someone."

Shane swallowed his asparagus. "You found a booth bunny?"

He was about to thank his aunt profusely when Melanie asked across the table—

"What's a booth bunny?"

He smiled, a bit sheepishly. He'd heard the term several times since his first forays into the wine business and took for granted it was used in America. Though it was likely an affront to feminists everywhere, the people who greeted and handed out wine to potential customers at these affairs were typically young women with sparkling personalities, knockout figures and very short dresses. He opened his mouth to explain, but heard a snort and someone else's voice answering in his stead.

"Booth bunnies are an attempt to sell a product by titillating the consumer instead of employing genuine marketing savvy or, heaven forbid, allowing the product to speak for itself." Audrey sliced the tip off an asparagus spear. "I took a marketing class called 'Sex Sells' at the J.C. It happens in all kinds of industries, of course, but it does seem particularly obnoxious when the product's value lies in a consumer's ability to discern subtleties. Nothing subtle about a booth bunny. Short skirt, big hair and a brain the size of a cork."

Emitting a snort of laughter, she popped the asparagus into her mouth and chewed. It took a moment before she realized she might have offended someone.

"Uhm, nothing personal against the girl you hired, Jenna. I just mean it's a screwy way to approach business." Another pause and she mumbled a sort-of apology to Shane. "Not that I mean *you're* screwy."

Of course not.

Shane harpooned a piece of salmon and stuck it in his mouth so he wouldn't be able to point out that the stick up Audrey's back was a helluva lot stiffer than the one she'd accused him of having.

He bristled without knowing precisely why her criticism bothered him so much. God knew he'd been under stress lately. He could use encouraging words, not potshots, while he worked his ass off building a business that would be the most important thing he had ever done in his life.

"Who'd you find, Mom?" Melanie asked, interested in the booth-bunny concept and either oblivious to the tension between her cousin and her friend or simply untroubled by it. "And how did you know where to look? What did you do, advertise?"

Shane noticed Jenna splitting her concerned glance between him and Audrey. "Why would I do that," she murmured, taking another sip of wine, "when I had a perfectly good candidate right under my nose?"

A large forkful of finely poached salmon had just gone into Shane's mouth when Thomas barked, "Who?"

Jenna smiled at Audrey over the rim of her glass, and every head turned toward the tomboyish redhead.

No! Shane thought, his gag reflex kicking in already. He'd explained the importance of these shows to his aunt. He was spending nearly the entirety of his personal savings on this trip. Audrey's derogatory comments aside, he could not imagine anyone—honestly, not a single woman of his acquaintance—less suited to a job for which she had to be unstintingly polite, charming and feminine than Audrey Griffin. Jenna couldn't mean—

"I think Audrey will make an outstanding booth assistant, don't you?" Jenna met each person's eyes briefly, smiling brilliantly and arching a brow as if daring anyone to disagree.

In that moment, Shane couldn't possibly have dis-agreed. He was too busy choking.

"Salmon bone," he managed to gasp, thumping his chest as Jenna, looking alarmed, rose from her chair. Across the table, Thomas rose also and took a step in Shane's direction. He tried to wave the help away. "I'm fine now."

They weren't listening.

Coughing into his napkin, he waved them off again, then realized that Melanie, too, had stood, her eyes round with panic. He followed her gaze.

It was Audrey who needed help.

Swearing, Shane leaped from his chair, shoving his aunt and uncle aside with an unfortunate lack of courtesy to get to her.

Grasping Audrey's shoulders, he turned her so that he could look fully into her face, now splotched a deep red.

"Are you choking?" he shouted into her face, making the international choking sign and waiting for her to mimic him before he commenced the Heimlich maneuver.

Instead of placing her hands at her neckline, she looked at him in panic and immediately reached for *his* neck, squeezing hard and nodding furiously.

"Let…go…" he commanded, prizing her hands off and turning her so he could wrap his arms around her with his fist under her sternum. He administered two swift upward pushes.

Nothing happened. Whatever had lodged in her airway had yet to budge.

Shane could feel Audrey's heart thundering like a dozen hooves and knew his was keeping pace.

"Come on, baby, give it up," he whispered in her ear right before he gave her diaphragm a shove that pulled her right off her feet.

Out flew a piece of grilled asparagus.

Impressed and enormously relieved, Shane released a breath and nodded. "Nicely done."

Chapter Five

Audrey coughed maniacally as she tried to catch her breath.

Shane's stone-solid arms were still wrapped around her. His murmured words tickled her ear.

Jenna was holding out a glass of water and looking worried. Thomas had his hand up, ready to thump her on the back should the need arise again, and Melanie had come around the table, an acutely sympathetic expression on her attractive face and a napkin in her hand. They all stood so close, Shane wouldn't have been able to back away if he wanted to.

Gently but firmly removing Shane's hands, still splayed across her stomach, Audrey accepted the napkin from Melanie, the water from Jenna and smiled to let Thomas know she was fine.

Then she eased away from Shane. He had saved her life. Too bad he, too, had almost choked upon hearing Jenna's plan. Kinda implied she was *not* a cute, charming girl, which put a big fat chink in her undying gratitude.

Involuntarily, Audrey's right hand covered her left. Somehow the Heimlich maneuver had made less of an impact than his squeezing her hand several moments ago. That had been earth-shattering.

Even now, she felt a swell of emotion that had nothing to do with the fact that she'd almost choked. That firm-yet-gentle, reassuring squeeze he'd applied to her hand was her undoing. She knew he'd meant it impersonally, but tears had risen to her eyes nonetheless. For a moment, just as she had last night, she'd felt…seen. Seen by Shane the way she hadn't felt seen by anyone in a long while.

And once again, she became aware of a place inside her that seemed comprised solely of painful raw need. She squeezed her eyes shut, wishing she could escape from the table and from her own feelings.

Humiliating, sentimental—

"Crap! You almost killed my best farrier, honey pie." Thomas lightened the awkward moment-after-near-death with a robust but humorous rebuke sent Jenna's way. "I nearly choked, too! Audrey can't go gallivanting around the world handing out wine samples. I need her here." He shot Audrey a paternal smile.

"She won't be gallivanting around the world." With a last glance at Audrey, Jenna returned to her seat and picked up the napkin she'd tossed next to her plate. "She'll travel to New York, Boston and Montreal. And she won't merely be 'handing out wine samples,'

Thomas. She'll meet and converse with people from many walks of life." Reaching for her wine, she spoke into the glass. "People whose interests extend beyond horses and racing."

Before he or Melanie could protest that people interested in horses and racing were the most interesting people in the world, Jenna insisted, "It would be good for her to get out and see something besides the inside of a stable."

Thomas's brows swooped down at the blasphemy.

"For pity's sake, Tom, sit back down and eat your lunch. Quest is my life, too. But Audrey has grown up here. She needs to expand her horizons."

Whether they recognized the determination in Jenna's tone or whether they actually agreed with her, Thomas and Melanie obediently resumed their seats. It seemed Audrey's brush with the ever after and Shane's lifesaving efforts were going to be overlooked by the Prestons for the moment in favor of hashing out Audrey's future. Without her input.

She and Shane were the only ones left standing. Awkwardly. As Thomas pointed out that he always worked Audrey's schedule around the classes she took at the local college, Jenna countered that classes did not substitute for life experience. Audrey realized that wishing she could disappear did not make it so. Doing the right thing, she turned toward Shane.

"Thank you. That was…very nice of you."

He took his time replying. "Don't mention it."

She thought she ought to say something more about how grateful she was, but he was holding out her chair, his gaze steady and calmer now. Longing to bolt from the room, she forced herself to sit instead.

Jenna had as good as stated, *"Audrey Griffin is a twenty-four-year-old woman who has spent her best years in a stable."* And the reason that truth ached so much was that she *did* want more—when she allowed herself to long for something. When she didn't deny the daydreams that sometimes came to her.

"Thank you so much, Shane, for helping Audrey." Jenna, usually the soul of grace, finally remembered her manners and remembered Audrey, too. "You are all right now, aren't you, honey?"

Audrey replaced her napkin on her lap, but knew she wouldn't eat another bite. "I'm fine. I'm terribly sorry."

"Nonsense. Don't you apologize." Jenna reached for her fork with a hand that shook slightly. "With everything that's gone on around here lately, I think I'm a little testy."

Melanie and her father exchanged a smile.

"I saw that." Sighing heavily, Jenna collected herself. "As you can see, Shane, Audrey is special to us. So thank you again." Her gaze, warm and wise and steely strong regardless of what was happening at Quest, settled on Audrey. "I've never heard you complain, but with all you've been through, isn't it time for you to do something for yourself? Something a little different?"

Audrey's cheeks prickled with heat, and she deeply wished Jenna had not referred, however vaguely, to "all she had been through." She had never asked for special treatment—not when she'd been ill, not when her mother had decided a sick kid was too much to handle and had taken a powder. And not when her father died; she'd returned to work two days later. Keeping busy had grounded her.

Eager to squelch once and for all time Jenna's strange proposal that she should accompany Shane to the wine shows, Audrey decided the time had come to discuss her plans. "I *am* going to do something new."

Her heart pounded. Though she never mistook the Prestons for family, they were the closest thing to relatives that she had left. The thought that she might disappoint them made her more nervous than it should have.

"I do want to travel." She nodded at Jenna and smiled sheepishly. "You could say I have a library of AAA travel guides. I was going to talk to you about it this week, in fact, but I suppose…I mean, since you've brought it up…I guess now's as good a time…" Her voice dwindled. Raising it above her trepidation, she ventured, "I'd like to start traveling by August. It's only the beginning of July, so I thought that would give you enough time to hire…hire someone new."

Well, she'd done it again: everyone at the table stopped eating. Forks remained suspended halfway to mouths; jaws went still and then slack. Even Shane, who likely had not expected this much drama with his noon meal, paused with his butter knife hovering over his roll.

Thomas recovered first, enough to practically bellow, "What the devil are you talking about? Travel if you want to, but you don't need to quit your job to do it!"

Resting a forearm on the linen-covered table, Jenna stared earnestly at Audrey. "Do you have other job prospects, sweetheart?"

"Other job—" Thomas began, and Jenna must have clipped him in the shin under the table, because he let out a huff and muffled himself into a frowning silence.

"No, no!" Audrey hurriedly assured them. Lord, she would never want them to think she was merely after a new gig in the same field. Especially not now. But if her doctor's suspicions proved correct, she would be little use to the Prestons anyway.

Jenna was watching her with an expression so motherly that Audrey actually felt herself almost tear up.

Though she wasn't at all sure she could swallow food, she took a small bite of her roll so she'd look casual and unconcerned when she said, "I'm not looking for another job at a stable. I'm just interested in traveling and exploring my options."

Jenna asked, "But what will you do for an income?" and Audrey sensed that everyone, Shane included, watched her, waiting for the reply.

"Dad left me a little money. I realize you'll have to hire someone else and that there might not be a job to come back to. But I've been thinking it might be time to explore other avenues. Outside of anything to do with horses," she hastened to add. "Like you said, I've been doing this most of my life."

"Yes, absolutely," Jenna murmured while her husband looked as if he wanted to pound some sense into the people around him. Jenna shook her head slightly, but he did not want to be hushed before he'd taken another whack at common sense.

"That's no plan at all, young lady! I know for a fact I don't pay you enough to gallivant around without a salary, especially if you have no job to come home to. I don't know exactly what Hank left you, but some of that—hell, most of it—ought to be rainy-day money. Besides, I give you group health insurance. That's nothing to sneeze at these days, and you need it more than most."

"Gee, Dad, if you wanted another kid to lecture, we could have invited Robbie to lunch." Melanie shot Audrey an apologetic grimace.

A thin veil of red covered Thomas's skin. "Everyone can use advice. Besides, she needs someone to…"

He mumbled the rest of his sentence, but Audrey was certain she heard, "…watch out for her now." She figured the others had heard the same thing, because no one contradicted him.

Appreciation swelled, full and bittersweet, inside her. For a single mad moment, the urge to unburden herself to the Prestons, to tell them about her visit to the doctor, to ask their advice and, even though it appalled her, to cry in their arms assailed Audrey.

Her next urge—one that seemed far superior—was to bolt.

Muscles seeming to move of their own accord, she stood, nearly knocking back her chair. She heard one softly spoken, Australian-accented word. "Steady."

With her heart pounding and perspiration beading across her brow, Audrey bunched her linen napkin in her hands, feeling stupid as hell; she realized she couldn't sit back down again without looking more like a basket case than she already did.

"Thank you…" Her tongue felt sluggish and thick. "Thank you for lunch."

Jenna visibly wanted to protest her leaving, but perhaps she recognized that Audrey was precariously close to losing control. The Prestons spent their lives working with a high-strung breed of horse, as deceptively fragile as it was strong. They knew when to push and when to let a wired filly blow off steam.

No one tried to stop her as she set her napkin next to her plate and turned from the table.

She wanted a clean path to the front door, but Shane stood to pull her chair aside. Their gazes locked like magnets. An expression of infinite understanding lit his eyes. Her mind, her traitorous mind, recalled the feel of his arms around her as she'd tried to catch her breath. Her skin began to tingle until it hurt.

She had to get out. Now.

Try as she might, she couldn't get the words *thank you,* or, really, any words, out again.

Gritting her teeth to keep from blubbering, she walked stiffly from the dining room, telling herself she'd think of a way to redeem herself later.

She walked through the beautiful home and into the strong sunshine. When the door shut behind her, it had the ring of finality. In the house, she left an unbroken family circle. Ahead of her was the life she'd been given to live.

Alone.

It had been three hours since lunch, and Thomas Preston still had indigestion. It didn't have squat to do with the food, which Eva and his wife had prepared perfectly, as always.

No, the problem was that lunch had been a reminder that everything he'd built—with blood, sweat and his whole damned soul—was changing. Without his permission.

He poured a stiff bourbon from the sideboard in his study.

"What are you having?" he asked without turning, his hand still on the crystal decanter of Kentucky's finest.

Brent, his second son and the best damned horse breeder in the States as far as Thomas was concerned, answered from his spot near the built-in bookshelves. "Nothing, thanks."

"Carter!" Thomas barked at his staff veterinarian, glancing at the tall, serious man who quite typically stood apart from the people with whom he shared the room. Thomas knew the separation was unconscious. He trusted Carter with his horses and his business, which was as good as saying he trusted the young man completely. "What'll it be?"

"I've got a couple of horses to check on when we're through here. I'll pass."

Grunting, Thomas continued with his plan to have an afternoon cocktail. He needed it. And when the two responsible, dedicated men behind him saw tomorrow's lead story on cable news, they would probably welcome a shot of whiskey, too.

Turning, he braced himself to ruin their day.

"I got a call from Nate Barkley," he began without preamble, because what the hell was the point of trying to soften what he had to say? "He was tipped that we'll be all over the news again by tomorrow night. Someone is breaking a story at five o'clock. It's full of bullshit about the team." To Thomas, the team was anyone and everyone on his staff.

"What else is new?" Brent moved away from the wall of books and lowered his long body to an armchair. Thomas noted the lines of tension and fatigue around his thirty-five-year-old son's mouth, and he didn't like it. "More veiled implications, no doubt."

Brent had never had an easy time in life. He'd always seemed to be fighting one thing or another—people in his youth and fate as an adult. His wife, Marti, had softened some of the rough edges and so had the arrival of their twin daughters. But Marti's death to cancer three years ago had been unbearable for them all. If Thomas could spare Brent this new blow, he would. Instead, he gave it to him straight.

"This time, the implications aren't veiled, son. According to Nate, the story will point unquestionably to Quest's breeder and veterinarian as the most likely people to have rigged Legacy's breeding. They're going to imply that you did it without my knowledge. The idea is that you're in competition with your brother Andrew to take over Quest, and you wanted to breed a champion at any cost."

Brent's blue eyes sparked with the righteous anger Thomas remembered only too well from his son's teenage years, and suddenly Thomas, too, knew an urge to come out swinging. An urge that he was sure rivaled anything his son felt. No one messed with Thomas Preston's family and got away with it.

He knew better, though, than to stir a pot of anger. Knew that the best way to protect his family and every employee for whom he was responsible was to appear calm, even if he wasn't.

"I've got our lawyers on it. If there's libel, the station will hear from us immediately." He divided a glower between Brent and Carter. "I don't want you—either of you—getting so riled that you do anything foolish."

Brent stood, the tension in his body seeming to ricochet around the room. "Is that all then?"

Thomas nodded, understanding that Brent had to get out of the room, to do something physical with the emotion inside him. More quietly he said, "That's it, son." He looked at Carter. "I've said it before—I'm sorry you're being dragged through this. All I can ask and all I can guarantee is that we stand together until the finish line."

With brown hair and blue eyes a bit lighter than Brent's, and with a much calmer demeanor, Carter nodded to both Prestons. "I'm not going anywhere."

Satisfied that he'd done all he could for now and aware that neither of the younger men wanted to sit around and chat, Thomas set his drink on a low, glass-topped table, shook hands and grasped each man's shoulder briefly.

He watched them leave, good men whose futures were at risk because someone—perhaps in his organization, perhaps outside—had decided to win at any cost.

Grabbing up his drink once more, he stalked to the window and looked out onto a land and a business that was his legacy, all he'd ever wanted. It had given him a past filled with integrity, pride and no small amount of gratitude and offered a future full of promise. How ironic that in between the past and the future stood a present that could make it all come tumbling down.

Chapter Six

"Holy crap! You couldn't find that bull's-eye tonight with radar. Of all the nights for me to partner up with you." Colby Dale slapped his thigh, staring in patent disgust at a dart that had missed its mark by at least six inches. "Sherlynn's birthday is coming up. I wanted to make extra cash so I could buy her the necklace she's been dropping hints about. Now I'll be lucky if I can afford dinner and flowers."

"If you're so concerned about Sherlynn, why aren't you home with her instead of playing darts and sucking down beer?" Audrey grumbled, surly as hell even though Colby was right that she couldn't control a dart to save her own life today. She couldn't control anything.

Shoving her hand into the pocket of her jeans, she

withdrew the cash she'd stuffed there before leaving her cottage and tossed it onto a nearby table. "That'll cover us both," she told the two men she and Colby had been playing against.

"I don't need you to cover me—"

"Well, I just did, didn't I?" she snarled, shaking off the hand Colby had placed on the crook of her arm and storming away from them all.

She shouldn't have come out tonight. Before she'd left her house, she hadn't wanted to be alone. Now she didn't want to be near anyone.

"Hey, Audrey!" Colby called after her. "Hey, I'm not really angry! Sherlynn's got more jewelry than she knows what to do with. Come on back." His plea was followed by similar requests from the others.

Audrey kept moving.

When she reached the bar, she ignored every empty stool until she arrived at the far end, where the bar curved to meet the wall. It was darker here than anywhere else in the lounge, and that suited her fine.

Herman was on duty. All she had to do was raise a finger, and he brought her a bottle of Michelob Light. He didn't bother with a glass or with conversation. She offered him a toast as he moved on to fill other orders. "To Herman, clairvoyant and psychologist rolled into one."

Taking an unladylike gulp of beer from the bottle, she grimaced. She'd never cared for carbonation, but beer was easy to order, low-cal if it was the light variety, and drinking it helped satisfy her wild streak.

Early on in her foray into higher education, she'd taken quite a few psychology classes at the junior college. She'd learned that where relationships were concerned, her emotional growth very likely had been stunted shortly after her twelfth birthday. She found it somewhat consoling that in most of her relationships, she was still only a preteen according to the textbooks. No wonder she continually alienated people and felt confused nine-tenths of the time. Theoretically she should still have a curfew.

"In Australia, when we go out, it's customary to order something we enjoy. You, on the other hand, clearly dislike beer, yet here you are drinking it for the second night in a row. Is that an American tradition?"

There was no point in hoping that the deep, ironic voice belonged to someone other than Shane Preston.

Reluctantly, Audrey looked to her left.

He wasn't laughing at her. Merely staring with that penetrating bemused curiosity.

"Last night I only had the whiskey," she told him. "No beer."

A brow rose and he inclined his head. "I stand corrected."

Like her, Shane stood to the side of his bar stool. Obviously neither of them was willing to commit.

"What's funny?" he asked when her mouth quirked.

"Just wondering what you're doing here."

"There's a tradition—I can't recall whether it's Chinese or Native American." He frowned. "Maybe it's Russian. In any case, once you save a person's life, you're responsible for it. I stopped by your home tonight. When you weren't there, I had a vision of you here at the bar again, choking on a maraschino cherry."

"I don't order drinks with maraschino cherries."

"Really?" He mock-frowned. "That's a bit of a shock, isn't it? You seem such a dainty thing."

The comment should have made her feel like a horrid oaf, but she saw the good-natured humor in his dark blue eyes, and she felt the impulse to laugh at herself. She allowed her lips to curl at the corners.

Briefly—as brief as she could make it—she had an image of him ringing her doorbell, her inviting him in and him stepping inside the small two-bedroom bungalow. She imagined Shane's subtly large presence would make the place feel tiny. And very full.

Perhaps Jenna had asked Shane to check up on her.

That thought was a bit depressing, so she made her smile as large as she could manage. "You know, I don't think that's a Chinese, Native American or Russian tradition."

"No?"

She shook her head. "I think it's from a *Star Trek* episode."

That drew the most spontaneous laugh she'd heard from him. "Even more valid then."

She had to ignore the tingles that the robust and utterly masculine laugh sent racing up her spine. She wasn't in the market for a life partner, but apparently that didn't make her immune to male energy.

"You're big on tradition," she murmured.

"Actually, I am."

Herman approached, and Shane surprised her by ordering two Irish coffees.

"The wine list here leaves something to be desired," he told her as Herman walked to the coffeepot.

Audrey couldn't liberate her mind from the fact that he'd ordered two drinks. Her gaze traveled the dimly lit lounge, looking for Shane's beautiful friend. Her mood took a nosedive.

"Wine's not tradition with Herman." She turned fully toward Shane, one elbow on the bar, as she attempted a posture that would look more relaxed than she felt. "So I'm fine. Thanks for asking. And thanks again for this afternoon. You're faster than the paramedics. I take it Jenna dropped the idea of my being your booth bunny after I left."

"You take it wrong. As far as I can tell, my aunt is more determined than ever to have you accompany me."

"What? Why? I would be a horrible booth bunny."

He didn't disagree. "Once you dropped your bombshell about leaving Quest so you could travel, you gave Jenna all the ammunition she needed. Even Thomas agreed that your traveling with me is a perfect compromise." He watched her speculatively. "They're very keen on your keeping your health insurance."

Audrey said nothing. Thomas and Jenna had seen her father's struggles when she became sick. He'd been more than grateful for his job at Quest; without it, doctor bills and time off from work would have ruined them.

"Maybe they're thinking of Brent's wife, Marti," she murmured. "She had cancer."

"I know. No one in my family had met Marti, unfortunately. You probably know that the Kentucky Prestons and the Australia Prestons haven't been close for years, although there are signs that is changing."

Glad to deflect the attention from her, Audrey nodded. "I knew that Thomas and Jenna had family in Australia and that the two sides of the family were estranged. But I don't know why."

"I'm not sure anyone can say why exactly. My uncle and my father are both strong, opinionated men. They each wanted to leave their mark on horse racing. One stable wasn't big enough for the both of them."

"Like Brent and Andrew," Audrey blurted before she thought better of it, realizing she might be speaking out of turn.

Shane's brows rose, but all he said was, "That makes sense. There's a certain amount of rivalry between my brother, Tyler, and me, too."

"I've heard about Lochlain." Thomas's brother, David, who was also Shane's father, had built the stable on a stake given to him decades earlier by his mother, Maggie. Lochlain was a powerful force in international Thoroughbred racing, though not as formidable as Quest. "You want to run a Thoroughbred stable? You're into horses as well as wine?"

"I'm not into horses at all. Couldn't care less." For a man who had just uttered the equivalent of heresy in the Preston family, Shane seemed pretty cheerful. "Tyler's running Lochlain now, and more power to him. Grapes and wine, on the other hand, hold more fascination for me than I would have guessed."

"Being a vintner is a new pursuit for you?"

He nodded. "Relatively. I worked at my cousin's

vineyard off and on as a kid. I learned a good deal, but the bug didn't truly bite me until last year. Now winemaking is my career. One that I care about very much."

Suddenly a veil came down, protecting his thoughts from her view. She'd bet a dollar to a doughnut that she could read them anyway. "So you'd like to hire someone more…let's see…appropriate?…to staff your booth at these wine shows."

She waited while he decided whether to answer honestly.

Shane didn't want to insult the woman. He really had sought her out to make sure she was all right physically and emotionally after the odd turn of events at lunch. She'd been on the verge of tears when she bolted from the room.

Then Jenna and Thomas had again expressed their concern that Audrey remain employed so she could continue to receive health benefits. Certainly he understood the value of health insurance, but she was young. Still in her twenties. He didn't want to dismiss their genuine concern, but neither could he allow their protectiveness to undermine his efforts here this summer. He had to make sure that Audrey found a way to travel without giving up her job at Quest—a way that did not involve him or the Cambria Estates wine booth.

"Irish coffees."

The bartender delivered two hot black coffees laced with whiskey and topped with whipped cream.

"Thanks, mate." Reaching for his billfold, Shane

placed several bills on the bar and picked up both coffees. "Let's get a table where we can sit down and talk."

"'Let's'?" Audrey's freckled nose wrinkled in her confusion. "You mean you…and me?"

He raised the drinks he'd ordered. "I suppose I can drink both. I'd rather not."

Her gaze darted around the lounge. Surprised, Shane asked, "Are you meeting someone?"

"What? Me? No, but I thought…" She pressed her lips together and shook her head, then led the way to a table against the far wall.

Shane followed, wondering what she'd been about to say.

Hilary had pointed out that "the redheaded girl" had wanted to dance with him last night. Even though he and Audrey had indeed noticed each other for a time, he hadn't taken the shared appraisal too seriously. Happened all the time in bars, and she'd started dancing with her jockey friend, anyway.

When they reached their table, Shane set down the drinks, intending to pull out a chair for Audrey, but she beat him to it, slumping down in the aged leather seat, her position almost aggressively casual.

Shrugging, he took the seat opposite and nudged a drink her way. "Do you like Irish coffees? Somehow I thought it would suit you."

"Why's that?"

Taking hold of the two thin red straws in his mug, he stirred the whipped cream into the drink. "Coffee's bitter, whipped cream's sweet—it's a drink fraught with contradictions."

She blushed and crossed her arms, and he wondered why the hell he'd said that. It wasn't what he'd been thinking at all. He tried not to smile at her scowl. "Sorry. I didn't intend to annoy you."

She shrugged her eyebrows as if the matter wasn't important enough for her to put her shoulders into it.

"You're private," he continued. "It upset you to have Thomas and Jenna discuss your personal issues in front of me, a total stranger, and I don't blame you. I am sorry, though, for the loss of your father."

She regarded him warily, like a cat invited by the neighbor's pit bull to share a meal. "Thank you."

"He was a farrier also?"

She gave him one nod. "The best."

"You're quite respected around here yourself. Thomas and Jenna are determined not to lose you."

She fiddled with her straws, but didn't sip her drink.

"You mentioned you've been collecting travel brochures. Where do you want to go?"

She responded slowly, tentatively. "There are a lot of places." Pulling the straws from the whipped cream, she put them in her mouth, licked them clean and ventured, "Some in the U.S. Some in other countries."

He noticed the bit of white froth left on her upper lip. It was quite a nice upper lip, he realized. "Well, if you ever go to Central America, I can give you some pointers. I worked in Guatemala for almost a year."

Her eyes widened with genuine interest. "What were you doing there?"

"Ostensibly working on a sewer project to improve conditions for indigenous peoples." His mouth twitched wryly. "Then there's the truth, which is that I was there more to help myself than anyone else."

"How so?"

His tongue was loose tonight. He hadn't admitted that—wouldn't admit that—to his own family. But now that he was thousands of miles from home and on the verge of a life that *did* have meaning, his fumbled past seemed less of a sin.

"Horse racing is in the Preston blood. But not in mine. I've spent a fair part of my life trying to find my future." When she frowned, he tried to clarify. "Looking for purpose, something I want to dedicate myself to."

She surprised him by laughing. "Maybe I should give you some pointers."

The dot of sweet white cream on her plump lower lip was distracting in the extreme. Whatever else she was, Audrey Griffin had an unconscious naturalness that was quite sexy. He tried to shake the thought from his head. "I'm waiting."

Gazing at him with an expression that could be construed as pity, she said, "You could spend your whole life looking for meaning and then be hit by a bus on your way to work. Just do something you enjoy."

It was suddenly too warm to drink the coffee. He set it aside and muttered, "I've heard that argument before. I prefer to engage in purposeful work while I'm waiting for your bus to mow me down."

"Well, there's a purpose to collecting garbage, so it's really not that hard to find a decent job," she pointed out practically, now using a red straw to spoon whipped cream into her mouth. "Anyway, you've got this wine gig, so you're happy, right?"

Wine gig.

"Let's talk about you," he said, because she was driving him crazy in more ways than one. There was another spot of whipped cream on her upper lip, which dipped in the center to form a gentle bow he hadn't fully appreciated before. He told himself firmly not to appreciate it now.

Shane planned to marry some day. As he was thirty-five, that day might arrive sooner rather than later. He wanted children; four sounded about right. The point was that he and his wife would build a family. He would build a business to sustain them all and teach his children by example the power of hard work, dedication and drive. If running a vineyard was not his children's passion, that would be fine with him and his wife.

When it came time to support his children's dreams, Shane would approve any healthful passion each discovered. Purpose—that would be the guidepost toward which he would urge them.

Despite the fact that none of his relationships had ended in marriage and family—yet—he was certainly past the fling stage.

So Audrey Griffin's lips were not his concern. All he cared about were her decisions—or to be more precise, one decision.

"If you enjoy living in the moment, you might want to include a cruise in your travel plans."

"A cruise," she murmured, appearing to consider the idea. "Have you been on one?"

He'd go crazy at sea with no intention other than to have fun. "No. I've traveled by boat—"

"To deliver medical supplies to an uncharted island off the coast of Borneo?"

Shane flushed. Normally, he didn't give a damn who approved of him and who didn't, with the possible exception of his family. Even then, it was his own opinion, his own integrity that counted in the end.

Hilary had been calling him a stick in the mud for over twenty years; it had never hurt his feelings before.

"It was educational material, and we were delivering it to an orphanage in Port-au-Prince, not Borneo," he informed her tersely.

"I'm sorry. I didn't mean anything—"

"Not at all." Forcing a smile that felt grim despite his best effort, he said, "We're on two divergent paths, you and I. Quite normal, isn't it, for two people to meet and have nothing in common? Odd, though, that my aunt is so determined for you to accompany me to the wine shows."

"Very odd."

"She and Thomas are a little overprotective where you're concerned." He couldn't help but allow some wryness in his voice. "You don't seem to require it."

"Damn straight."

"Right then. We're agreed that our working together is a bad idea. I think we can also agree that it's up to you to put a stop to it."

"Whoa." Audrey had loaded her straw with more whipped cream, but instead of putting it in her mouth, she flipped it towards him, splattering the front of his very nice Tommy Hilfiger shirt. "Sorry."

Pulling her napkin from beneath her drink, she handed it to him. "Why is it my responsibility to tell Jenna her idea is whacked? They're your wine shows. And she's your aunt."

"Precisely," he said, dabbing at his shirt. "I don't want to offend her by trying to prove that the idea is, as you aptly point out, whacked. You, on the other hand, can put an end to this simply by telling Jenna you've decided to travel somewhere you've always wanted to go—just make sure it's not Boston, New York or Montreal—and that you will return to work when you get home. You'll fulfill your objectives to take a break from work and to see someplace new without forfeiting your job or benefits. And neither of us will have to insult my aunt."

"Uh, hello? Mr. Has His Own Agenda? Maybe you weren't listening up at the big house when I said I want to travel for a while without worrying about when I need to come back. I wasn't talking off the top of my head. I've given it plenty of thought, and I don't want to be tied down. I may come back someday...or I may never."

He thought of Hilary, and the idea that anyone would take security for granted or tempt fate sent a flare of anger shooting up his body.

"Seize the day all you want to, but have a little common sense. Nobody is safe without health benefits."

She shook her head. "Health insurance doesn't keep you safe."

"It's better than playing Russian roulette." He glared at her. "And if you talk this way in front of Jenna and Thomas, you've as good as waved a red flag in front of a bull."

"Well, once I give my notice formally it'll be a done

deal. Jenna and Thomas might not love my decision, but they won't blame you for a thing. What's that phrase from the land down under? 'No drama, mate.' Once I'm out of the picture, you can hire the perfect bunny for your wine booth."

Cursing beneath his breath, Shane passed a hand over his eyes. "Dear God, you are stubborn. All right, do what you want with your future, but wait until the wine shows are under way. Give me a week before you turn in your notice. That way I can find someone else, without Jenna pressuring either one of us."

Her skin was so smooth and sprinkled with such an abundance of freckles that she looked like a little kid when she scowled.

Shane wagged his head. She reminded him of the dolls Hilary had insisted they play with when they were children.

There had been one with freckles, a long red braid— he remembered, because he'd tried to trim it with a hunting knife—and an expression he recalled as mutinous, as if she hadn't wanted to play with a boy any more than he'd wanted to play with a doll.

Perhaps this was a lesson in fate for him; redheads were bound to cause him trouble.

He sighed. "Kindly say what's on your mind. There's nothing more chilling than staring an enemy in the face and having no idea when she's going to strike."

Chapter Seven

Audrey did not consider herself Shane's enemy. And she wasn't planning to strike. But she was upset.

Perhaps "upset" wasn't strong enough. Pissed. She was pissed. He didn't have to keep rubbing it in that he didn't want her near his booth.

She understood that wine shows, like wine tastings, required more grace than an afternoon in a stable or a night at Herman's. She figured that a successful booth bun—booth assistant—should possess, at bare minimum, a knowledge of grapes and wines in general, as well as those of the specific vineyard she was representing.

"Do you grow Barbera vines at Cambria?"

Shane looked at her, bemused, just as she wanted him to.

"Barberas," she said again, slowly and clearly. "Do you grow them? I'm just curious, because I know the Barbera's neutral aroma allows it to blend well with more distinctive varietals, and of course the vines are so adaptable and fungal resistant and all. I was just wondering. And, yeah, I'll hold off giving Thomas my formal resignation, but I'll wait five days, no longer. I want to give Quest a few weeks' notice. So you'd better get cracking if you're going to find someone who can fill all of your requirements."

Which would read, she thought, wishing she didn't feel so bitter, like a list of traits belonging to a Miss America contestant. He would look for someone beautiful, someone charming, someone with teeth whiter than God's robes. Perfection. Everyone wanted perfection.

"I'm going home." Abandoning her coffee and whatever was left of this conversation, she said, "I've got a lot of packing to do if I'm going to be out of my cottage by the end of the month."

She pressed her palms against the table's edge, intending to rise, and was caught off guard when Shane's fingers clamped around her wrist.

"Wait. How do you know about Barberas? About the vines?" The deep-sea eyes, so right and so startling against his sandy hair and tawny skin, narrowed as if he'd somehow been betrayed. "Jenna never said…"

Audrey laughed. "Don't let it bother you. We both know I'm still not the right person for your booth." She longed to ask why he didn't use the woman he'd been with the night before. The utterly feminine, genteel-looking brunette. Damned if she'd admit she'd been watching him, though.

Shane shook his head. "How do you know about wine? For most people, wine knowledge begins and ends with whether they prefer Merlot to Cabernet." When she attempted to pull her wrist free, he tightened his hold. "Answer me. Please."

Audrey sighed. "I take night classes. One was on wine production. The teacher was big into viticulture. It's no big deal."

She looked pointedly at her wrist. He let go, and she tried not to feel disappointed.

Crossing swords with Shane Preston was the most exhilarating thing she'd done in months. Maybe years. That was pathetic.

"Thanks for the coffee."

His lips parted, but he apparently thought better of what he'd been about to say and merely nodded.

She stood.

Awareness, excitement, unholy irritation, resentment, gratitude, yearning, need—in the two days that she'd known Shane Preston, she'd felt more than she'd allowed herself to feel for years. For better or worse, she liked the roller coaster of emotions she experienced with him.

His hand was on the table now, but the memory of his touch circled her wrist like a bracelet.

"Good luck at your shows," she said gruffly, knowing she had no reason to see him again before he left.

He pushed back his chair and stood, a move that looked strictly polite, but then he stared down at her in the disturbingly intense way that made her stomach buzz.

"What is it about you?" he murmured. "You're the most maddening girl. You don't do anything easily, do you?"

It was an honest question, his tone and gaze curious.

Lord, she wanted to stay at the bar with him. She didn't want to play pool or darts. She didn't want to shoot the bull over beers or shots. She wanted to dance, but not wildly, as she so often did to blow off steam or to distract herself from feeling sad or lonely.

Right now, she wanted to hear a slow song, one as moody as she felt. She wanted to be in Shane Preston's arms, just as sad and scared as she truly was. She wanted to feel his strength and his caring, because she knew already that he cared about people, whether he liked them particularly or not.

She wasn't looking for love, not from him, but she couldn't help imagining the comfort of feeling less alone for a night

And then the image of a lovely brunette filled her mind.

A smile—wry, self-deprecating and a little wistful— curved her lips. "No." The word emerged in a whisper. "I don't do anything easily."

She turned and walked from the bar in long, ground-eating strides. As soon as she got home, she would plan her trip. She would see places she'd never seen, meet new people, laugh as if nothing bothered her and sing even if she didn't know the words. And she would try to fall in love—really hard and really fast and with absolutely the wrong person. For a little while. It wouldn't be easy to plan an affair into the itinerary, but she would try. An affair that would elicit the riotous, intense emotions that made her feel alive.

The emotions she felt when she was with Shane.

Two days passed, during which Audrey saw nothing of the man who continued to invade her thoughts. She pored over her travel brochures when she had downtime. She had promised Shane she wouldn't quit for several days, so she was still in a holding pattern.

Much, however, had transpired to change the atmosphere at Quest and, potentially, all their lives.

A cable sports show had eagerly discussed the questions that loomed around Leopold's Legacy's paternity and the integrity of Quest Stables. The program's anchors had suggested that the true parentage of a prize-winning stallion could not be a mystery to the horse's breeder or veterinarian, even if one "assumed" the animal's owner had been left in the dark.

Though individuals in the Quest organization were not named, Audrey furiously hoped Thomas would sic his lawyers on the reporters just the same. Everyone in the racing community knew that Brent Preston and Carter Phillips were the men whose reputations were being maligned.

The mood at Quest had taken a serious plunge. With rumors of a North American ban by local and regional racing commissions on majority-owned Quest horses looming, two more owners announced they were transferring their animals elsewhere to avoid any association with Quest's problems. With fewer horses in the stables, there would be less work, and unless the mystery of Legacy's sire was solved, Quest's training program would also suffer. The stable's stud program would be as good as dead.

Which meant that not even loyalty to Thomas would keep everyone in his or her job. One groom had already bolted for greener, less turbulent pastures. More employees would follow. How many people would stick around, unsure of how the scandal was going to play out, unsure of who was going to be implicated?

Moreover, if Legacy's sire was not a Thoroughbred, as originally believed, the Prestons would forfeit all of his winnings, including those from this year's Kentucky Derby and the Preakness.

Audrey felt fiercely loyal to her employers. It seemed unfathomable that they could lose their status as one of the great Thoroughbred stables of all time. She feared, however, that their situation was going to grow worse, not better, until someone discovered how a viewed breeding between Apollo's Ice and Courtin' Cristy could result in a champion racehorse whose sire was not, in fact, Apollo's Ice.

In the interest of loyalty, Audrey was glad that she'd postponed her resignation. If her own crisis were not pressing down on her, she would never leave the Prestons at this time.

So gloomy was the atmosphere at Quest that she was glad for an excuse to escape the stable for a while on Monday and drive into Twisted River.

Slipping her ageing Ford Ranger into a parking space in front of Ace Hardware, she picked up a half pound of nails and a new pair of gloves. She was standing on the street in front of the store before she remembered she wasn't going to need new gloves. Her old ones would last until she left, and even though working with horses was the only job she knew, her future was a big question mark. There was no telling if she'd ever shoe a horse again after she left Quest.

A sheen of perspiration covered her forehead, and her heart thumped hard enough to hurt. It happened every time she contemplated her future.

Rather than heading directly back into the hardware store, Audrey walked along the hot sidewalk, looking in store windows, trying to imagine what an average young woman of twenty-four would be thinking and doing right now.

Immediately, Shane's image came to mind.

Pausing before the large picture window of an upscale clothing boutique, Audrey gazed at a mannequin wrapped in a sundress the color of vanilla buttercream. The bodice was snugly fitted, the skirt a luscious flow of overlapping layers so that it seemed to swirl even while remaining perfectly still. She could hardly take her eyes off it.

Her father had bought her a prom dress once, but she'd felt awkward and unsure of herself, and since then, she'd stuck mostly to pants. Now she imagined how she might feel in a dress that evoked images of garden parties and gentle breezes and one very intense, very approving gaze.

As if God were reading her mind at that moment and reminding her not to covet someone else's oxen, the door to the dress shop opened several feet away, held by a saleslady who told her customer in a tone that was perhaps overly gracious, "You come back again, honey. Have a real, real good day."

Audrey stood transfixed as the brunette she'd seen with Shane emerged, not walking, but rolling a wheelchair awkwardly over the bumpy threshold.

The brunette's biceps tensed from the strain of maneuvering the chair. Her beautiful face grimaced in what Audrey recognized immediately as self-disgust.

Aware that she was staring, Audrey quickly retreated until she was tucked into the doorway of the adjacent store.

The wheelchair got stuck, and the saleslady stood by uncertainly, finally reaching for the handle nearest her.

"I've got it!" The warning was half snapped, half grunted as the woman in the chair used all her strength to give the wheels a mighty shove, finally propelling herself onto the sidewalk. "Thank you," she muttered to the saleslady, who was holding the door.

Bobbing her head and saying something Audrey couldn't hear, the saleslady hustled back into the store, leaving the woman alone on the quiet street.

Alone, except for Audrey.

Shane was nowhere to be seen, but to Audrey his presence loomed. His companion that first night—the perfectly stunning woman Audrey had envied—was in a wheelchair. She wore no cast or brace on either of her legs, which were positioned primly side-by-side, feet motionless on metal footrests. The chair appeared to be permanent.

But she was not used to it.

Gut instinct had never been Audrey's strong suit, but she trusted it this time. The woman's expression conveyed the resentment, mortification and confused resignation Audrey had felt as the only kid in her school who saw more doctors than she did teachers. Whatever had happened to put this stunning woman in a chair, it hadn't happened long enough ago for her to stop fighting it.

Reaching around the back of the chair, she uttered a frustrated cry, then curled her hands into fists and pounded them on her lap. "Damn it!" she said, loudly enough for Audrey to hear. Then she lowered her head and released a sigh that would move the hardest heart.

Audrey forgot about being envious or even curious. Leaving her spectator's post, she walked up the block.

"Excuse me…"

Without knowing exactly what she was going to say, she remembered how horrid she'd felt when people had treated her with pity or excessive care. She'd always preferred the practical approach of the nurses, who when they saw a need, addressed it simply and directly. Pretending someone wasn't sick or in a wheelchair was like ignoring the proverbial elephant in the room.

She kept walking until she was abreast of the other woman. "I'm Audrey," she said. "Can I give you a hand with something?"

The woman raised her head in surprise, suspicious eyes so deeply hued they looked like bluegrass. Standing so close, Audrey saw that the woman's skin was as smooth and milky as porcelain. She looked like the character from some wonderful tragic novel, but Audrey knew that comparison would be unwelcome.

Aware that she was going to refuse her help even though it was sorely needed, Audrey got down to brass tacks. "I can never keep my sh—" She stopped and grinned. "My stuff together, either. Looks like you need help finding something, but if not…" Shrugging, she kept her smile in place. "That's cool."

Maybe thirty seconds passed, during which the blue-grass gaze stayed glued to Audrey. "I forgot my purse in the dress shop." The young woman spoke softly and with an accent Audrey recognized. It was Australian, like Shane's.

"Hmm." Audrey nodded, glancing toward the glass door. "I wouldn't want to maneuver through there twice. If you tell me where you think you left it, I'll go look." She swung her small backpack around and dug through to find her wallet. "Here." She held it out. "Hang on to this. So you'll know I won't run out the back with all your loot."

A reluctant smile, half amused and half self-mocking, gave Audrey a hint of what Shane's friend must have looked like when her smiles came more easily.

"I'm Hilary." Setting Audrey's wallet on her lap, she maneuvered her chair so that she was facing Audrey directly and could extend her hand.

Audrey took it and shook with her customary strength. After a brief flare of surprise, Hilary returned the grip as heartily as she could, which wasn't bad given her lithe frame, but she was no weight lifter.

Feeling much weaker than the average teen, at fifteen, Audrey had worked with weights and started running to gain strength and endurance. She thought Hilary could use some physical training in order to push her chair with more ease.

Uh, definitely not your business, Griffin. Just get the purse and be on your way.

"Be right back," she said, heading into the store.

The purse was perched on a low table bearing a jewelry display, next to the cashier's desk. Audrey explained herself to the clerk, scooped up the shoulder bag and returned to where Hilary was waiting, a curious furrow between her elegantly arched brows.

"Audrey," she said, as if she were testing the name. "I remember seeing you at a pub the other night. I can't remember the name of it."

"Hot To Trot."

"Yes! And…you work for Quest Stables, is that right? Shane has mentioned you."

Audrey nodded, not wanting to let on that she'd noticed Hilary at the bar, that she had practically memorized the other woman's face. Or that she'd been lusting over Hilary's boyfriend. She easily recalled her first impression of them: perfect man picks perfect girl. Same old story. Now she had to reevaluate everything she thought she knew about him. She'd be up all night.

"Well. Good to meet you." She raised a hand and backed up a couple of steps. Briefly she wondered why she hadn't seen Hilary, or Shane for that matter, around the estate. There were guest rooms at the main house and cottages kept for company. "I hope you enjoy the rest of your stay in Kentucky."

"Oh, do you have to go?" Hilary laughed self-consciously. "I mean, Shane's been my only source of conversation since we left Oz. And let me tell you, I am tired of discussing grapes and tannins and the effect of oak aging. I could use some girl talk, and I wonder…" She bit her full bottom lip. "You've been so kind, and Shane knows you, so we're not total strangers."

Audrey sensed what was coming next and tensed.

Hilary smiled winsomely. "We could have tea. Shane and I are staying in a motel up the block. There's a little restaurant next door, so we could go there. Or we could stay in the room. I prefer that actually. There's a coffeemaker, not very fancy, but I brought tea with me, and we've got packages and packages of the best biscuits in Australia. Do you like sweets?" She grimaced. "I'm babbling, I know. It's just—" She released a huge, heartfelt sigh. "You're the first person in ages who's treated me like a normal human being, even though you didn't ignore the hardware." She thumped the arm of her chair.

Audrey didn't have to get right back to work, so felt churlish saying no, but having tea with the girlfriend of the man she'd been obsessing about seemed in very poor taste.

"I'm afraid my cousin and I have been getting on each other's nerves." Hilary pursed her delicately bowed lips. "Either he wants to go out and I want to stay in, or vice versa. Another person for tea would be a relief to him, too, I'm sure."

A car honked in the distance, but the only sound Audrey was clearly aware of was the noise from the blood rushing through her brain.

"Who's your cousin?" The question spilled from her lips in an overly urgent squeak. Hilary tilted her head.

"Shane, of course. You didn't know? Oh, but I suppose he wouldn't have had any reason to mention me, would he? And I've been keeping to myself, maybe a bit more than I should." She wrinkled a nose much smaller and more elegant than Audrey's. "Sorry. I've been prattling on as if you know who I am. You probably think you stopped to help a madwoman."

No, Audrey thought, but she was suddenly a whole lot happier. And thirsty.

"I do have some time," she ventured. "What exactly are the best Australian biscuits ever?"

"Tim Tams, of course. And they're even named after a Kentucky Derby winner." Hilary grinned and reached for the wheels of her chair. "The motel is a couple of blocks up."

Chapter Eight

She pointed herself in the correct direction and began pushing. Audrey walked along by her side, carrying her bag of nails.

"I got a manual instead of a motorized chair," Hilary grunted, "because I wanted to stay in shape. And I didn't think I'd be in it that long. It's been a year, though, and I have calluses on top of calluses, so the joke's on me."

They were moving along at a pretty good clip, and Audrey didn't think Hilary wanted help, so instead she asked, "Why are you in the wheelchair?"

Hilary glanced up. "I like people who are direct."

"Me, too."

"I was in an accident a year ago. In my parents' vineyard. We were riding a tractor, and it overturned into a ditch." Her voice caught only briefly as she continued. "They died instantly, so they didn't know what happened to me. In a way, that's a blessing. On the other hand, I can't tell you how many times I've wished for them to be here. It doesn't matter how old you are, I suppose. When something awful happens, you want your mum and dad so you can cry like a baby."

Audrey faltered. She fell out of step with Hilary, who looked back at her. "You all right?" Frowning, she stopped and turned the chair to face Audrey. "You're not all right." A shrewd and distinctly bitter expression darkened her eyes. "I don't usually talk about it. Most people get uncomfortable. They want me to be the brave tragic figure or the happy paraplegic who thinks it's just dandy to wheel everyplace. You seemed—"

"It's not that. I'm not uncomfortable because you're…you." Audrey caught up to the wheelchair, standing far enough away so that Hilary wouldn't have to crane her neck to look up. "I get it. I do."

Hilary's gaze became penetrating, probing. The kind of gaze a person adopts after they've experienced hardship of a personal nature. The kind of gaze that seeks to determine, *Are you friend or foe?* Audrey had seen that look often on the ward of the children's hospital she'd been in. She remembered talking to the friends she'd made in the hospital about "them"—the normal people—and "us."

"I had cancer," she blurted. "Twice. When I was a kid. And my parents were divorced, and…" She shook her head. "It's not exactly the same, I know. But I get it."

She almost never, ever told anyone, but she was glad

she'd said it now. Glad in the way she had been glad to talk to Brent when his wife was ill. Glad in the way she would be to talk to his daughters someday if they wanted to ask questions about their mother's experience, to ask her what it felt like to have cancer or to be scared to die.

At first Hilary looked stunned, then grateful, then emotional, as if she might start crying. She began to move the chair again. "Come on. Let's get drunk on the best chocolate biscuits Australia has to offer and complain about our incredibly difficult lives."

An hour and a half later, they had shared war stories about embarrassing hospital moments involving good-looking young doctors and hospital-issue gowns, the horror of bedpans, the frustration of dreadful food and the way they had protested—Audrey had flushed a greasy chicken leg down the toilet; Hilary had planted a wilted salad in a potted flower. They also compared notes about how they had lain in bed at night, silent and sleepless with the suffocating fear that life after their hospital stay would never, ever be as good as life before.

Audrey had never spoken so easily to anyone, not even her father, for whom she had tried to be brave and hopeful so he wouldn't worry. Hilary put on a similar front for her family. She said Shane was the rock they all leaned on.

"He was so wonderful. He was in Central America when the accident happened, and he came home immediately. My grandparents were a wreck. Shane took over."

Hilary had maneuvered out of the wheelchair so

they could both sit on the bed to eat cookies and drink cups of tea they made in the motel room's tiny sink-top coffeemaker.

"He came to the hospital every day so my grandparents wouldn't have to shoulder all my care, and then he moved in with us to help keep the vineyard going. He's been learning all he can about running the place. He's such a perfectionist." Hilary set an uneaten cookie on a Kleenex. "He was born with a silver spoon in his mouth, but he spit it out at the first opportunity. He does things the hard way, that boy."

Her eyes focused on a point across the nicely appointed room. The animation in her face yielded to a grave stillness. "He never makes me feel like a charity case, or as if I'm his project, but the accident gave him a reason to stop wandering for a while." A corner of her mouth lifted wryly. "I suppose I'm less objectionable than a sewer project."

Audrey understood. "It bothers you that he's made you his mission."

"No. It bothers me that I'm letting him. I haven't done much this past year. Moped a little. Worked at gaining back some strength. Bought into the illusion that I'll walk again."

Audrey had been half reclining along the foot of the bed. Now she sat up. "What do you mean? Is there a chance—"

Hilary began to shake her head hard, her lips compressed. "For a while this year, I walked with braces and crutches. But the pain was too much." Her eyes welled with tears. "I needed more surgery, so I could get through the day without tranquilizing myself into a stupor. They warned me that the surgery could leave me chair-bound, but at that point all I could focus on was getting through the day without sobbing." She rubbed at the moisture beneath her lashes. "I'm still not doing a very good job at that."

Audrey leaped up, pulled the box of Kleenex out of the dispenser in the bathroom and sat on the bed again, handing the tissues to her new friend.

Hilary smiled gratefully, blowing her nose with a loud honk that broke the tension and made them both laugh.

"The vineyard isn't doing well at the moment," she confided with a sigh as she tossed her balled tissue into a wastebasket Shane must have wedged between the bed and the end table for his cousin's convenience. "We didn't have the money for me to come to America, but I've always wanted to, so Shane insisted. And he 'happened to hear' about a neurosurgeon in New York who's been working miracles with people like me. 'Happened to hear.'" She shook her head. "I bet he researched for a solid month and then coerced the doctor into seeing me the same week as the wine show. So I'm going with him to New York. And if he gets his way, I'll probably be under the knife again before the end of the month."

She spoke lightly, or tried to, but Audrey sensed the fear and grief.

"You don't want more surgery? Even if there's a chance?"

The tears started again and Hilary reached for the Kleenex. "Oh, bugger! I hate being weepy." She sopped up the tears, took the deepest breath she could manage and looked Audrey squarely in the eye. "Maybe, if they could tell me how much of a chance. But what if this—" she gestured toward her legs "—is me now? The longer I put off accepting that, the harder it is. And to be in the hospital again, this time so far from home…" She shook her head as if she loathed considering it. "But if this surgeon gives us even a little hope, how do I refuse? I know my grandparents are desperate for good news."

Hilary's confusion and her dread of further intervention was palpable.

"My doctor thinks I might have cancer again," Audrey blurted. "If I do, I don't want more treatments. Not unless they come with a money-back guaran*damn*tee."

Hilary's eyes widened with shock and concern at Audrey's sudden revelation. Audrey felt her own mouth opening to form a wide O as she, too, reacted with surprise. She hadn't intended to say that aloud. To anyone.

Now that she'd blurted it to Hilary, however, it felt…okay. It felt like a giant relief, actually, to talk to someone who understood that invasive medical treatments carried an emotional as well as physical price tag. And that the emotional toll was sometimes more overwhelming than the physical.

"I'm so sorry." Hilary reached across the bed for Audrey's hand and squeezed hard. "When will you know for sure?"

"Well…" Audrey decided not to tell the whole truth this time. "My doctor wants me to have a biopsy. Fairly soon."

Immediately was the word Dr. McFarland had used, but Audrey saw no point in sparking additional questions. She wasn't ready to get the biopsy yet.

"If you don't take the treatments, what will you do instead?" Hilary asked.

She shrugged and took another cookie. "Go to Hawaii? I've always wanted to learn the hula."

Hilary let go of Audrey's hand, struggling to lean forward and grab the cookie before Audrey took a bite. She fell onto her side, holding up the sugar-laden snack. "This is terrible for the immune system." She pushed herself back up. "Okay, I know this might sound hypocritical, but shouldn't you plan on getting treatment no matter what? I mean, cancer's not like paralysis. People heal, and then they're fine."

Audrey sighed. "I don't know what treatment options would be available to me. I've already had enough radiation to light up half of Lexington. If it's a recurrence of what I had before then there's probably not much they can do except focus on life extension, and life on chemo sucks, so what's the use?" She pointed. "I want that cookie back."

"Nuh-uh."

They reached for the package at the same time, but Hilary got there first, crushing it slightly as she held it up.

"Ha!" She put the extra cookie inside and tucked the package behind her pillow. It crinkled loudly as she settled back. "So if it's not the same kind of cancer, then what?"

Audrey sighed. "Then it depends. On a lot of things," she added before Hilary could ask, "and I don't want to talk about it, because we don't even know and there are way more interesting things to discuss."

After watching her a moment, Hilary nodded. "I

think I had an identity crisis after several months of being in hospital. I forgot who I'd been before I was the girl in 301B. Being a professional patient is confusing."

"Like you've come to a stoplight and are standing still," Audrey agreed. "The light turns green and everyone around you starts walking, but you can't move."

"Yes."

Both women were quiet for a time until Audrey asked, "Why aren't you and Shane staying at Quest?"

Hilary glanced down at her lap, looking sheepish. "That was my decision. His aunt and uncle did offer. And I feel terrible, because I'm costing us money." When she looked up at Audrey again, she seemed to be asking for understanding. "I didn't want to face all the questions. Or the disappointment if the surgeon can't do anything. It's easier to deal with my own feelings without having to put on a company face, if you know what I mean."

"Yep. Gotcha." Audrey smiled and they shared the quiet camaraderie neither would be able to find with the average woman her age.

Audrey couldn't envision going through chemo and radiation again, not because of the puking, fatigue and what the manage-your-chemo pamphlets grossly underestimated as "discomfort." It was that edging so close to death was unthinkable without her family to urge her on.

Before, she'd lived for her parents. The first time she became ill, she consciously fought to stay alive because of them.

The second time, she consciously fought to stay alive to spite one of them.

"So about your travel plans," Hilary ventured,

touching on one of the other topics they'd covered. "Would Montreal, Boston or New York figure in?"

Audrey had no plans to accompany Shane to the wine shows, but before she could say so, someone knocked on the door.

"Who is it?" Hilary called.

"It's me," came the Aussie-accented baritone, "the handsomest and most amusing of your cousins."

Rolling her eyes, then winking at Audrey, Hilary responded as if she were thrilled, "Come in, Tyler!"

A key card unlocked the door. "That wasn't funny," Shane said as he entered the room. "Just for that, I may not share my new discovery—"

He stopped so abruptly upon seeing Audrey, it was almost comical.

The knowledge that he was single and not a superficial horse's ass did scary things to her heart, like make it start and stop randomly.

Hilary said, "Tyler is Shane's brother, and he's dreamy. All the girls for miles around think so."

"All the females for miles around Lochlain have four hooves, a mane and a tail," Shane grumbled automatically, the teasing obviously so many years old they didn't even have to think about it anymore.

"So what is this discovery of yours?" Hilary asked, and Shane's gaze shifted from Audrey, whom he'd yet to greet, to his cousin.

"I think I shouldn't tell you," he said dryly, "but in the interest of proving that I am, in fact, a knight in shining armor…" He opened a paper bag and withdrew four tiny individual-size cartons of Ben & Jerry's.

"Ice cream," Hilary groaned, putting her hands over her stomach. "We can't eat it."

"You can. Each carton comes equipped with its own miniature spoon." He seemed so impressed by this fact that Audrey found him quite adorable, not an adjective she'd have considered using to describe Shane Preston even a few hours ago.

Hilary pulled the package of cookies from their hiding place behind the pillow. "We broke into these—" she glanced at the digital clock on the nightstand "—almost two hours ago. This was pack number two."

He winced on their behalf. Walking behind Audrey, who was sitting up straight on the foot of the bed, he moved to the round Formica table near the window and set down his booty. "I bought four of these. Two for Hilly and two for me, so I can either eat them all or I can share." It was the first comment he directed to Audrey.

She didn't even think about the massive amount of sugar she'd already consumed. She simply wanted to stay in the room, to remain where Shane was and to feel the pulse-thumping excitement she experienced around him.

She held out her hand. "If you have Phish Phood or Cherry Garcia, I'll take that."

"No!" Hilary held a hand out, too, but hers commanded *stop*, not *gimme*. "Don't give her ice cream, Shane. She had chocolate biscuits. You'll be contributing to the destruction of an immune sys—"

She stopped when she caught the panicked look Audrey threw her. She frowned then appeared to understand.

"Of a perfectly good figure," she finished. "Women don't work it off as easily as men."

Seating himself at one of the table's two vinyl-covered chairs, he held a carton aloft. "You're afraid of this tiny thing?"

Dressed in jeans and a sky-blue T-shirt that stretched across muscular chest, rock-solid shoulders and flat abs, he rested his right ankle on his left knee and opened the lid of a Wavy Gravy.

"So how did you two meet?"

Hilary gave him a thumbnail sketch of their encounter on the street, quite obviously making Audrey sound like far more of a Good Samaritan than she actually had been. Then she looked at her cousin accusingly. "You didn't tell me that the Audrey Griffin, who Jenna wanted you to hire, was the girl from the bar."

He fed himself ice cream with the spoon he'd detached from the lid. "It seemed immaterial."

Hilary snorted. "Immaterial? You were eyeing each other like you wanted to do it on the dance floor."

Audrey's head swiveled toward Shane, then Hilary, then back to Shane. He spluttered a nice spray of Wavy Gravy onto his shirt and swore.

Spying the Kleenex box, he stood, grabbed several tissues and mopped his T-shirt. "I would like to finish one meal in the U.S. without choking."

Chapter Nine

When Shane looked up, he met Audrey's gaze and her heart beat like a hundred thundering hooves.

So she'd been right? He had been attracted, or at least interested, that first night at the bar? She'd convinced herself she had completely misread him that night.

A shiver ran across her arms as she mentally ticked off the facts as she now knew them. He wasn't a horse's ass. He wasn't shallow. *He really had been staring at her.*

She recalled easily how good his attention had felt before she'd assumed Hilary was his girlfriend. She remembered the rush of excitement. The absence of fear, for those precious few moments. She wanted more of that feeling.

None of her few boyfriends had been the caretaking type. None had made her feel sheltered and protected, even temporarily. And that was fine; she hadn't wanted that from them. In the past, she'd chosen her relationships based on how simple they would be to conduct—and how easy to end without anyone getting hurt.

If she got to know Shane well enough to feel his embrace, the feelings would be exciting, but not simple. The end of their relationship would hurt.

Audrey shook her head clear of her thoughts and met Shane's contemplative gaze. He would be in the U.S. only a short time…

"Any luck on the booth assistant?" Hilary asked, then winked comically at Audrey. "Otherwise known as the bunny hunt."

Audrey glanced at Shane to see him wince. "I will not use the term booth bunny again as long as I live." He drew an X over his heart. "I need to hire someone with wine knowledge, grace and courtesy. And I need to do it yesterday. It's not easy." Sitting, he reapplied himself to his ice cream, pausing before he put the tiny spoon in his mouth. "If either of you plan to say something likely to make me choke, please speak now or forever hold your peace."

"So no luck then," Hilary concluded, returning to the topic.

Shane answered, "No," reluctantly around a mouthful of ice cream.

"Hmm." Hilary wrinkled her perfect features into a troubled frown. "I've been hoping this would all be taken care of before we left for New York. I don't want to worry about Cambria while I'm seeing this new surgeon of yours and taking tests."

Immediately Shane put down the ice cream. "You don't have to worry. I've got everything covered. The only thing I want you to do on this trip is sightsee and talk to Dr. Nichols."

"Yes, but still."

Hilary nibbled her thumbnail. "We leave in three days, and I was hoping to tutor whoever you hired so she'd know about Cambria's wines specifically. If you don't find someone soon, I suppose I'll have to assist you in the booth."

"You said you absolutely didn't want to."

"I absolutely don't. But Cambria is my business, too. Of course it would be far too stressful to work in the booth *and* deal with Dr. Nichols and his tests and whatnot, so I'll have to cancel—"

"Over my dead body!" Shane rose from the chair like a sea god. "He's booked months in advance. I had to call in markers halfway around the globe to get this appointment. You are not canceling." He stabbed the air in her direction. "Seeing Dr. Nichols is more important than working in the wine booth."

"Well, if you say so." Hilary expelled a thoughtful sigh. "But I don't know how we'll pay for medical insurance unless the shows are a success."

"I don't want you to worry about that."

"Easier said than done." She shook her head unhappily. "No. Unless we find someone to learn about Cambria and work in the booth—and I mean sooner than immediately—I will bite the bullet and be your booth bunny on wheels."

"Hil—"

"I've been sitting here too long. I'm getting stiff." She gathered the scattered tissues, deposited them in the wastebasket, brushed the cookie crumbs off the bed and said, "Audrey, my dear new friend, would you be so kind as to give me a hand here?"

"I can—" Shane began, but Hilary waved him off.

"We've been doing just fine all afternoon."

Audrey knew exactly what Hilary was doing. A couple of days ago, this morning even, she'd have put a stop to it. But now… Now she felt jittery and lightheaded and good, and it wasn't only from the sugar.

"Sometimes," Hilary continued as Audrey wordlessly fetched the wheelchair and helped Hilary move safely off the bed, "another woman is the best comfort."

Settled in the chair, Hilary looked up, her lips parted as if she'd surprised herself with a sudden thought. "Audrey! If you were our booth assistant, then not only would I be able to relax about who was helping Shane, so I could see the surgeon, but you could also do some sightseeing with me. Shane wants to see the Statue of Liberty, Ellis Island, that sort of thing. I need someone to shop Fifth Avenue with me."

"Hil, you know I'll—"

"Someone who will actually enjoy it. And—" she lowered her voice "—it would be nice to have a woman around before and after I see the doctor. There are things women understand, Shane, which men don't. Especially a woman like Audrey."

Audrey's heart played "Reveille." She prayed that Hilary would stop right there, before mentioning anything specific. She didn't want to talk to Shane about her illness. If she went to New York and Boston and Montreal, then she wanted Shane to think of her as an average, ordinary...booth bunny.

Of course, there was the not-so-little fact that he currently looked as if the top of his head might blow off while he tried to come up with a way to get out of hiring her.

For her wine-appreciation course at the junior college, she had attended one wine show and discussed its mechanics with her instructor.

So many of the booth assistants she'd seen that day had been good-looking, sexy and charming as heck. Audrey had not met a single one who was a farrier by trade, who had callused fingers and short unpolished nails, or who looked as if she owned more Bag Balm than lip gloss.

Therefore, she couldn't really blame Shane...too much...for looking as if he'd stuck his finger in a pencil sharpener. She tried to think of something to say that didn't sound defensive.

"Look, I may not be a 36-DD, but at least I have more gray matter than silicone." The remark wouldn't win a blue ribbon for graciousness, but she figured he'd have to admit she had a point.

Shane's expression remained unreadable, but his gaze dropped to her 36-B bosom, currently clad in a sturdy Maiden Form bra and one of the button-down shirts she preferred atop her jeans.

"It's not the best time to decide this," he concluded.

"It's the only time," Hilary countered. "We're supposed to leave for New York in a few days. You told me your aunt was peddling the idea of Audrey working with you, but I'm sure there's still some kind of notice that has to be given."

He turned toward his cousin. "You realize this needs to be a business decision?" His modulated tone was a low, cautionary rumble.

"Of course. That's exactly why we need to begin as soon as possible. We'll have to tutor Audrey about Cambria."

Once again his gaze swept her. No longer guarded, his expression said plainly that they'd have to tutor Audrey about a lot more than their vineyard.

"She can't look like that."

Hilary waved a dismissing hand. "I'm already on it."

"Hey, I'm right here!" Audrey folded her arms and glared. Talk about insulting. "I haven't agreed to work with you," she said for Shane's benefit. "I have plans of my own. Although—" she narrowed her eyes to show him she meant business "—*if* I were to decide to help you out, you'd be damned lucky to have someone who knows the difference between a Riesling and a Sauvignon blanc, so don't get all 'Ee-ew, she doesn't look like Pamela Anderson' on me, because I can carry on an intelligent conversation with any damn person who walks up to your godforsaken booth."

"Without resorting to epithets?"

"That could be a challenge," she admitted, "if you keep pissing me off. And who says 'epithets'?"

They both turned to the sound of Hilary clapping her hands in glee. "This is going to be so much fun!"

Chapter Ten

Seamus snored on the sofa alongside Audrey, his belly full and his tongue sticking partway out of his mouth, as a program about a family with sixteen children concluded on The Learning Channel. Squeezing a plastic bottle of caramel sauce onto the remains of a giant silver mixing bowl of popcorn, Audrey idly read the bottle's label and shuddered.

"High fructose corn syrup, sugar, yellow number five. Yeesh." The stuff could kill her. It and the popcorn had been her only dinner, and she was beginning to feel nauseous.

She set the container of caramel sauce on the coffee table and licked her fingers, but the thrill was gone. Dr. McFarland had left another message on the machine, urging her to keep her appointment with the surgeon who would perform the biopsy. Audrey had deleted the message.

Throughout her misspent adolescence, she'd lived as wildly as she'd dared, which had basically amounted to trying cigarettes a couple of times, sneaking one of the Thoroughbreds out for a midnight ride, and pedaling her ten-speed over the old ramps Robbie had constructed for his skateboard. She recalled a very specific feeling that had pumped through her like blood when she did something foolhardy: a spectacular, buzzing sense of triumph, as if she'd beaten life, instead of the other way around.

Now she ate junk food to thumb her nose at fate. She was considering a trip to the kitchen for butterscotch morsels when someone knocked on her front door.

"Company," she told Seamus, thinking that Brent might have decided to stop by. The day before, she'd left him a message saying she had a few boxes of hand-me-down toys, including one of collectible horses, for his girls. Her toys and collectibles, once treasured keepsakes because her mother had given her many of them, had been boxed up and collecting dust in a storage shed for too many years. Time to pass them on. She needed to start traveling lighter.

Licking her teeth to make sure all the caramel was gone, she opened the door. Shane stood on the threshold, looking too large for the small cottage entrance.

"Oh. Hi."

Dressed now in an ivory button-down shirt over khaki trousers, he presented the very picture of the casual yuppie-about-town. Smelling of soap and aftershave, he must've changed for dinner with Hilary.

She was still in her jeans and white shirt, but was barefoot now and afraid she smelled like Seamus. She assumed Shane thought so, too, when he leaned toward her and sniffed the air.

"What is that?" he asked with the accent that, truthfully, made her think of movie stars and sex.

"It's Seamus."

"Seamus?"

"My dog. Well, not *my* dog. Thomas's."

"Ah, Seamus, the dog. That's not what I smell, though." He sniffed again. "It's popcorn, but there's something else. Caramel?" He arched back and looked at her with his head high and his eyes narrowed to accusing slits. "You have caramel in there?"

"Uhm, yeah."

"I want some."

Audrey stared dumbly. She'd left the motel room that afternoon shortly after swearing at him. He'd smirked as if she'd proved his point: if a job required grace and charm, she wasn't the best candidate.

She took a step back, bewilderment trumping any other feeling. Shane stepped past her, glancing around the cottage as she closed the door. When he saw Seamus, who had roused himself enough to place both front paws on the coffee table and his head in the popcorn bowl, Shane stopped and cocked a brow at her.

"I've heard you Americans treat your pets like family."

"Seamus!" Audrey jumped forward to remove the popcorn bowl. "Paws off!" She swept his huge feet off the coffee table. He stood with his front paws on the carpet, his rump still on the sofa and kernels of caramel corn stuck to his black-and-gray beard.

Shane came over to peer into the bowl. "Was that all of it?"

"Yes."

"Too bad." He raised his head, gazed at her long enough for Audrey to feel the reckless impulse again, and nodded toward the TV. "You have a couple minutes to talk? Or am I interrupting?"

No matter how stuffy and annoying he could be, Shane was gorgeous, and she didn't care for the fact that the current setup in her cottage looked grim, no matter how you sliced it: single woman in her twenties spending the evening home watching TV with— borrowed—dog the size of a Toyota.

She gestured helplessly toward Seamus. "He comes in through the window at night."

"Is that a fact? A secret admirer then." Shane winked.

Good job, Audrey.

Allowing his hind paws to slide to the floor, Seamus spared Shane one wary glare then padded heavily down the hall.

"That's Thomas's dog, right? Where's he going?"

To bed, but Audrey figured she'd have to be on laughing gas to admit that she let a one hundred-and-sixty-pound dog sleep in her bed so neither of them would be lonely.

She shrugged. "Maybe out the window again."

He watched the dog go, then gestured to the vacated couch. "May I sit down?"

"Sure."

Audrey noticed the bits of popcorn and Seamus hair

on her sofa cushions and grabbed Shane's arm. "Take the chair."

As he changed direction, she saw the sticky fingerprints she'd left on his shirt.

So did he. Glancing at his elbow to check the damage, then shooting her a not-unpleasant, ironic look, he took a seat on her father's recliner and smiled politely. "Well, I'll get right to it then, shall I? You, Audrey Griffin, are the booth assistant I've been waiting for. Would you do me the great service of accompanying me to wine shows in New York, Boston and Montreal? All expenses paid, negotiable salary and a guaranteed job, whether you want it or not, when you return home. In addition, the job comes with a wardrobe allowance."

Audrey looked down at her plain, stable-sturdy attire. Several caramel drips streaked her shirt and she felt her face go as red as her hair. When she glanced up again, Shane held up a hand, a wince already forming on his handsome face.

"Before you tell me what to do with the plane tickets, let me assure you that was not a slight. The wardrobe budget is actually Jenna's offer. She intends it as a gift."

A gift for a woman who didn't know how to dress like a female.

Audrey rose to put the caramel sauce in the kitchen and wash her sticky hands. The floor plan of the cottage was open, so she couldn't escape entirely, but at least she could hide her face while she sorted through her feelings.

She'd spent her teen years in a stable with a father who was a farrier and no female relatives to guide her.

She hadn't attended school much at a time when girls helped each other with makeup and hair and such things. She should have asked someone, maybe even Jenna, for advice long ago, but pride had stopped her.

Rather than trying to compete in a game with indecipherable rules, Audrey had told herself long ago that makeup was a mask; fancy clothes an artifice. She'd assured herself she was above that sort of thing.

This was the first time since her early teens that she could remember wishing she'd picked up a fashion magazine every now and again.

Without glancing to see where Shane was looking, she put the caramel sauce in her refrigerator and took out a carton of milk. She poured a tall glass then opened a cabinet to retrieve a package of Nutter Butters.

Thinking better of serving the cookies in their package, she pulled a salad plate with a grapevine motif down from a shelf. Arranging the peanut butter cookies on the plate, she carried it and the milk into the living room.

When she dared to look up, Shane was watching her.

She set the dish on the square oak table by the chair, needing to nudge aside a framed photo of her father standing next to Leopold's Legacy. Her dad had bought her a long pink satin dress when she was sixteen. The satin had been shiny with stiff puff sleeves, and the pink had clashed awfully with her hair. She'd thanked her dad profusely and hid the dress in the back of her closet, where it had stayed until a spring-cleaning Goodwill run a few years ago.

Shane helped without speaking, taking the glass from her. She stepped back and straightened.

"Do you have Nutter Butters in Australia?"

He reached for one of the sandwich cookies, imprinted with a waffle pattern to resemble a peanut shell. "I don't know."

"They aren't fancy, but they'll stick with you."

He looked at her instead of the cookie. "A lot of things that aren't fancy stick with you."

She flushed with shock and pleasure, then chastised herself. He wasn't really flirting; he wanted something.

Moving to the couch, she brushed off the cushions Seamus had dented, then realized she was too restless to sit. She turned toward Shane, crossing her arms over her chest.

"So what's up? One minute I'm the last person on the planet you want to involve in your business, and the next you're at my house, asking me to be your booth bunny and fake flirting. What's that about?"

Shane returned the cookie to the plate and set the milk beside it.

He wore his inscrutable expression again—the one that made him look mysterious, sexy and implacable—as he stood. He walked until only the corner of her family's old, battered coffee table stood between them.

"I was not 'fake flirting.' You have stuck in my mind. Hilary was right, I did notice you that first night at the pub. How could I not? Beating those blokes at pool, dancing like something wild. You're impossible to miss, Audrey Griffin."

He took her chin gently between his fingers. Audrey couldn't breathe at all. His voice lowered until she had to focus all her energy on listening. "I heard your toast at the bar that night. 'Live for today, for tomorrow we may die.' I've never felt that way. I believe in futures. I believe in planning."

She barely recognized her own breathless laugh as she tried to lighten the moment before her heart pounded right out of her chest. "You know what they say. 'Man plans; God laughs.' Maybe it's better to be spontaneous."

The pad of his thumb played across the freckles along her jaw. "Spontaneity," he whispered, "is the right of men with no responsibilities."

"That sounds like another quote. What about 'The best laid plans of mice and men'?"

He shook his head, a wry smile making him more handsome than ever. "We are completely different, you and I. Seems pointless to deny that opposites attract."

His thumb stilled on her skin. He moved again until mere inches remained between them. His head lowered, just a bit.

After days of uncertainty and racing thoughts, it was nice to know one thing with crystal clarity: she wanted him to kiss her. She no longer cared whether it was right or wrong, smart or foolish. She raised her arms to circle his neck and stood on tiptoe to reach his mouth. They wound up meeting halfway. Hunger and need contributed to a kiss more blisteringly sensual than any she had ever experienced. Ever, ever.

The hand on her back pressed her closer, flattening her breasts against his chest. His free hand cupped the back of her head, his fingers thwarted by her braid when he tried to thread them through her hair, and a corresponding, frustrated growl rumbled low in his throat.

She was aware of the way he kept his tongue strictly out of the action until the last moment, and even then his exploration was brief, almost reluctant, as if he couldn't help himself.

She didn't have much experience with romance. All her relationships had been based on physical need, not love or true passion, but she understood this: Shane didn't want to want her. It made sense, she thought, as the kiss ended and he stepped away, his hands falling to his sides. He was rational; he planned things. He hadn't worked this into his U.S. itinerary.

Predictably, he began to rationalize. "That was… wrong of me. Under the circumstances—"

"I kissed you."

That stopped him for a moment.

"I kissed you," she said again, shrugging as if it were no big deal even though her heart was still doing somersaults. "Anyway, what are the 'circumstances'?"

She didn't feel really bad until guilt edged his eyes and pulled at the corners of his mouth. Regretting a kiss was one thing; feeling guilty about it…that was bad.

"There's no future in a relationship between us," Shane began, the words emerging slowly, heavily and with great care. "I wouldn't want to hurt you by misrepresenting myself. I'm here for a specific purpose. And only that purpose."

Audrey smiled to herself. At least he didn't say he wasn't attracted or that he had a girlfriend in Australia. He was merely revealing another facet of the sobermindedness she found both intriguing and frustrating.

"Do you mean you're here in the U.S. for a specific

purpose," she asked, getting back to his comment, "or here tonight for a specific purpose?"

"Both."

"Okay." In a sudden move, she plopped herself on the couch and smiled. "So talk to me. I know why you're in the U.S. and I can guess why you're here. But I think I'd like to hear you stumble your way through it."

"You think I'm going to stumble?"

"After making it clear that I'm not even remotely your idea of a booth assistant? I think there ought to be at least a little stumbling, yeah. And if that kiss was about buttering me up—"

"You kissed me."

Right.

"Okay. So go ahead. Tell me why you're here. Throw in something about why a no-strings affair would mess up your agenda. Oh, and would you toss me a couple of Nutter Butters while you're standing up?"

Chapter Eleven

It was not like Audrey to be offhand about sexual matters, but Shane's stunned expression was so satisfying she thought she might try to make a habit of it while he was around.

After a moment's hesitation he turned to pick up the whole plate of cookies plus his glass of milk and returned to the couch, where he sat beside her. Placing the plate on his lap, he took a cookie and started munching without offering one to Audrey.

She knew exactly what he was doing.

"A gentleman always shares."

Slowly he wagged his head. "Maybe I'm not a gentleman. You want one so badly, come and get it."

He spoke as casually as she did, and although he wasn't smiling, she saw the humor deep in his eyes.

She produced a heavy, overburdened sigh. "The truth is I've had *way* too many already. And those—" she glanced in the direction of the plate "—are really pretty average."

Neither wanted to break first. They stared at each other while he tried to think of a comeback, but in the end, his mouth twitched. Before she knew it, he'd thrown back his head and was laughing—a big, chest-deep laugh that made the couch vibrate.

"You win." He passed her the plate. "Have a cookie."

She took one of the Nutter Butters, though she'd never felt less hungry—or more exhilarated—in her life.

Setting the plate between them on the sofa, he gazed at her with frank curiosity. "I haven't decided yet whether you're as bold as you like people to think you are."

Caught off guard, she insisted, "I don't care what people think of me."

He scowled, but there was no anger. "Everyone cares what others think, Audrey. Sometimes we rise above it. But unless you're a hermit, you have to establish a satisfying way to fit into your environment."

"Fit into your environment? Is that like growing to the size of your aquarium?" She shook her head adamantly. "Some people will never fit in. If they spend their entire lives worrying about it, then they may as well be hermits, because they're going to disappear anyway."

"Do you fit in?"

She decided to tell the unvarnished truth. "Not even a little bit."

He looked at her with blatant curiosity rather than pity.

"I haven't decided yet whether you're showing off or you're fair dinkum."

"Fair what? Did you just call me a name?"

He laughed. "I said fair dinkum. It's slang in Oz for genuine. Real."

"Oz?"

"Australia."

"Oh." She grinned. "Most of the time, you sound pretty normal."

"Most of the time, I omit the slang. When in Rome."

Audrey tilted her head quizzically. "When in Rome…what? Pretend you're somebody else?"

"Now, don't spit the dummy at me, Miss Griffin. If I spoke strine all the time, it's London to a brick you'd think I had kangaroos loose in the top paddock."

His accent became far more pronounced for the Crocodile Dundee lesson.

"Okay." She laughed. "But isn't it a lot of work to pretend you're someone else?"

"I don't have to pretend. I was educated in England. Speaking the Queen's English—with an Aussie accent—comes naturally, and since then, I've traveled around the world. I find it more enjoyable to establish a common ground than to beat people senseless with my individuality."

"You speak other languages then?"

"French. Spanish. Enough of one or two Mayan languages to get by. And a smattering of Italian that would allow me to order a decent meal in Rome."

He spoke without bragging, but Audrey was deeply impressed.

"I took two semesters of French at the junior college. But then I saw a photography class I wanted to try and I didn't have time for both, so I put off taking the next level. But I would love to speak another language. And travel."

"It sounded the other day as if you've got your travel plans well in hand." He popped most of a cookie into his mouth and took time to chew and swallow before speaking again, his expression growing more sober as he approached the true reason for his visit. "So you're a woman of many interests. You've studied French, photography and wine appreciation?"

"Among other subjects."

"Did you enjoy wine appreciation?"

"I was aces in my wine course."

Moving the plate of cookies to the coffee table, Shane turned fully toward her, his expression more serious than she had seen it yet. "Hilary is scheduled to meet with a surgeon in New York."

"She told me."

He nodded. "Did she also tell you that up until today she was resisting the notion of going through with it?"

"She mentioned a reluctance to visit more doctors. If there's no point." Audrey spoke carefully, not wanting to betray Hilary's confidences, but interested in Shane's perspective. And he was quick to give it.

"She's in a wheelchair. If there's a chance—any chance—that she can walk again, we're going to take it."

He spoke so assuredly that she knew immediately he could pressure Hilary into having surgery that she didn't want or for which she was not ready. He would do it with the very best of intentions, but the effect would be the same—a woman pressured into being a patient when what she wanted and needed was to find herself again.

Audrey decided to probe a little, but as gently as she could. "'We'?"

His brows swooped down.

"You said, 'If there's a chance, we're going to take it.' Don't you mean 'Hilary'? *She's* the one taking all the chances."

Instantly, tension filled his body. "What are you saying?"

Hmm. Apparently not gentle enough. She backpedaled, reluctant to create a problem for her new friend. "I'm only saying that sometimes just living is preferable to spending all your time fighting for something."

This time the quirk of his mouth was unappealingly sardonic. "Seize the day."

Audrey felt frustrated then realized she was being unfair to him. He might have traveled the world, but he'd never wandered the corridors of a hospital, wondering if he'd ever again race through a field on his way to nowhere or have a dance or a first kiss.

"Well, anyway, you were going to tell me why you're here," she prompted.

After a moment, he nodded.

"When I walked into the motel room, you were the last person I expected to see. I came in prepared with my bag of tricks to make Hilary smile, to find a spark of the joy she used to have. I didn't expect to see her with a new girlfriend, laughing. You accomplished in an afternoon what I haven't been able to all year."

"Sometimes it's a woman-to-woman thing. I'm sure her friends can—"

"No." Shane sat forward on the edge of the couch. He rested his elbows on his knees and looked straight ahead while he spoke. "Hilary rode in steeplechases. Most of her friends are from that world. They're off dealing with their own lives and when they visit they seem at a loss for how to relate to her." He cracked a smile and shrugged. "I try to be entertaining, but apparently you're better at it. She came alive this afternoon. She's interested in going to New York for the first time. Interested in the vineyard again."

He stood, paced several feet away, turned and gazed down at her with a challenge in his eyes. "I'll pay you double what I intended to pay anyone else. I'll need you at the shows all evening, but we'll arrive in each city a day early, and you'll be free to sightsee."

"You're really prepared to settle for me?" she goaded, though she wasn't truly offended. She already knew what her answer would be, and money had nothing to do with it.

"You're not the usual, but I'm counting on there being at least a few dresses in your wardrobe. I also hope you can manage a civil attitude toward every bloke who comes within twenty feet of the booth. As for your wine appreciation course, hopefully you'll be teachable."

Audrey's jaw dropped open a bit more with each word that fell from his lips. He was as honest in his estimation now that he wanted her as he had been when he'd choked over the idea. "You're not even attempting to flatter me. Make an effort, at least."

"Flattery would annoy you. I'll give you the truth instead. I interviewed several beautiful girls, but not one of them knew a Shiraz from a Chardonnay. And I was bored during the ten-minute interview, whereas you, Audrey, have managed to make me feel many things, but boredom is not one of them." As he spoke, the tension seemed to drain away, replaced by a growing conviction. "You're what we need. Say yes."

She smiled. "Out of curiosity, because it's really not going to affect my answer, how much is double what you intended to pay anyone else?"

He named a figure. Surprised, she whistled. "I'd have done it for half, but I'll take it."

"You'll take it?" His hands came to rest on his hips, his head cocked as he made sure he'd heard correctly. "You're going to be my booth assistant?"

"You had me at 'You're not the usual.'" She stood, acutely aware of the well-loved jeans that rode her round hips, of her boxy shirt—plain white except for the caramel drips—and her large bare feet and serviceable, unpolished toes. Giving him a good look at what he'd just hired, she approached him and stuck out her hand.

"Really looking forward to peddling your grape juice, Mr. Preston."

Shane used his key card to enter the motel room adjoining Hilary's. It was only nine o'clock, but the light was out in her room and all was quiet.

He'd considered stopping somewhere for a cup of coffee, but had wanted to be nearby in case Hilary was awake and in need of anything. Tossing car keys, key card, and his wallet onto the dresser, he began to undress en route to a shower. He felt restless enough to consider opening one of the bottles of wine they'd brought with them to the motel.

The touch of Audrey's hand had sent an electric shock up his arm.

For the past few years, Shane had deliberately confined his romantic liaisons to those with a limited shelf life. He'd been traveling, working. There hadn't been space in his life for anything permanent. Now he knew he'd be settling in Hunter Valley, the home he'd rejected years ago in pursuit of a meaningful life and to which he had returned, as sure as a man could be of his place in the world. He was ready to give himself to something lasting.

God willing, his next relationship would be a glorious beginning. Part of a future with roots that would reach deep into the Hunter Valley soil, planting the seeds of a legacy he could leave to his own children.

The woman for him would share his goals. She would dream similar dreams. Anything else would surely end in dissatisfaction for one or both of them, and he didn't believe in disposable marriages.

He and Audrey Griffin, who wanted nothing more than to enjoy herself one day a time, would be a terrible match.

Entering the bathroom, intent on drowning his restlessness beneath a blistering hot shower, he examined the unexpected attraction he couldn't seem to shake.

Beneath her near-swaggering brashness, Audrey reminded him of a kitten standing firm against a bulldog—back up and fur on end as she spit warnings, but scared and pliant on the inside and waiting for someone to scoop her up and pet her until she purred.

Turning the squeaky hardware in the shower, Shane laughed. "The Kitten" would have his privates on an anvil if she heard him describe her like that.

Stripping off the remainder of his clothes, he acknowledged that, perversely, the things he liked best about her were the obvious contradictions. She talked about not caring for anything beyond the present moment; yet as he considered the facts, he realized she was one of the least laissez-faire individuals he'd ever met.

She cared so much about her employers that she had trouble leaving them in their current circumstances. This afternoon, she had come to Hilary's aid. Her take-no-prisoners free-spiritedness was at odds with her concern for others.

Stepping into the shower-tub combo, he lowered his head to let the pounding spray soak his hair and sluice over his shoulders.

Why wouldn't his bloody mind let go of Audrey Griffin?

In the year he'd been at Cambria, he had realized that being a vintner suited him much more than raising horses ever had. Yet when he thought of Audrey, he pictured a filly—not a Thoroughbred, but a wild and restless mustang.

Grabbing the motel-issue shampoo, he dumped a fair amount on his wet head and scrubbed vigorously.

There were always variables in making wine. A seasoned vintner could influence the product in ways both subtle and obvious. Control. He liked it.

When he looked for a woman again—and he would—she would be a fine wine, not a wild filly. She would be steady, dependable. Together, they would be the brick and mortar of the family.

He and Audrey Griffin were unsuited to each other. Furthermore, she was now officially his employee. Strictly, one-hundred-and-ten-percent off-limits for the duration. Their handshake should have acted like a dousing of ice water.

Since it obviously had not, Shane grit his teeth, reached forward and turned on the cold water. Full blast.

Chapter Twelve

Prior to leaving for New York, Audrey had purchased a Fodor's Guide, which she'd read like a novel. She'd Googled the hotel in which they were staying, printed photos and made a personal itinerary for sightseeing on her day off.

She'd decided that she wanted to see the Statue of Liberty, the Empire State Building and Times Square. She'd read that nineteen million people populated approximately fifty thousand square miles and that so many nationalities were represented, one could barely count them all. She'd learned that the Finger Lakes region was home to the state's fertile vineyards, and she'd realized that one day of being a tourist would be like choosing only lettuce at an all-you-can-eat buffet.

Still, no amount of research prepared her for the loud, frenetic, gorgeous reality of New York City. The glut of cars and people, the variety of architectural styles and the myriad fascinating things to look at kept her head swiveling in the cab on the way to the hotel.

Beside her, Hilary was more quietly interested in the city. In the front seat next to the cabbie, Shane, who had been to New York before, appeared to be focused more on his thoughts than the view beyond the car.

As Audrey settled into her hotel room, her mind returned again and again to the plane ride from Kentucky.

For the first thirty minutes, she'd sat next to Shane, who had seated himself beside Hilary. The women had conversed by leaning across him. The fifth time in a half hour that Hilary passed Audrey the current issue of *Harper's Bazaar* and said, "Look at that dress—that would be brilliant on you," Shane had clamped a hand around his cousin's wrist, returned it and the magazine to her lap and made Audrey change places with him.

Thus, for the remainder of the trip, Audrey had pretended an interest in haute couture while concentrating mostly on the solidness of the left arm that brushed against her right.

When Hilary wasn't exploring Audrey's shopping options, she and Shane tutored Audrey in the subject of Cambria Estates Vineyard.

Hilary had been born on the vineyard, but it was Shane's voice that quickened with interest, *his* eyes that sparked with passion as he described the undulating green hills of the Hunter Valley wine region, the rows upon rows of Shiraz and Riesling and Chardonnay grapes that would be turned by methods both complex and subtle into the wines he hoped would make Cambria one of the world's premiere wineries.

"One of the world's premiere wineries?" Audrey had teased. "Not just Australia's? Pretty ambitious, aren't you?"

He had taken the question seriously.

"We'll focus on the national market, of course, but a ripper wine shouldn't remain a secret treasure. By combining our grapes with fruit grown on other soil, we can explore unique blends and still remain true to our region. What's good for Cambria will be good for Hunter Valley."

"You had to ask," Hilary had mumbled to Audrey, laughing affectionately at her cousin. "You've got to know by now, Audrey, that Shane doesn't do anything by half measures. He plots and he plans and then when he's sure he understands absolutely everything about a topic—pow! He takes over the world."

Audrey had glanced at Shane, adding her laugh to Hilary's when she saw him glower.

"I'm not trying to take over the world," he'd argued. "I'm trying to improve it. When you taste our rosé," he'd told Audrey, "you'll see what I mean. It crosses all borders. It's fruity enough to be a good aperitif, but deep enough to accompany meat. I expect the rosé alone to put us on the map, so you'll have to get to know it well."

"She's going to drink it, not marry it," Hilary had cracked. An intense and, Audrey thought, fascinating tutoring session had ensued.

She'd learned that Shane could forget his surroundings when discussing his passion, and that the sharp edges of his intelligence and ambition were warmed and softened by a true concern for community. He cared about his effect on the people around him.

He was affecting the heck out of her.

"Wine is the true whole food." Leaning toward her in the cramped coach seating, he spoke with mesmerizing conviction.

"How's that?" Audrey had murmured back, conscious of Hilary comically shaking her head in the seat to her left. In that moment, however, nothing could have distracted Audrey from the impassioned, beguiling intensity in Shane's deep blue eyes.

He used his hands quite a lot when speaking about a topic he loved. "The soil not only feeds and supports the vines, it's responsible for different nuances among same varietals of grapes. So first—" he held up a finger "—we have the earth, sun and water contained in the glass of wine. Then we have people—community. Humans are the only animals that drink wine, and generally they do so among friends, with good conversation involved. Wine comes from the earth, quenches the thirst, feeds the human soul." He had three fingers raised. "How many things can you say that about? As of this year, all our grapes are pesticide-free by the way."

Audrey had murmured appreciation of the commitment to organics, but truthfully, she'd been stuck on the image of Shane and a collection of good friends sitting on a beautiful patio overlooking the vineyards, sun sparkling off crystal goblets, people laughing and conversing at a table laden with food and drink and companionship. At the head of the table was Shane, relaxing with a woman's chair scooted close to his. They held glasses of wine, of course, and the woman's head rested against his shoulder as she listened to the hum of voices and the children's laughter...

Audrey had gone silent. Then Hilary had said wryly to Shane, "You've scared her half to death, boomer, with your religious conversion to the god of wine." She'd elbowed Audrey in the ribs. "Don't mind him. He's gone dotty since he caught the wine bug."

Shane's grin had been sheepish, but proud, too. Audrey would have smiled back, but the vision she'd had of life at the vineyard had disturbed her too much. She'd clearly seen the woman next to Shane: auburn hair, freckles, an expression of inexplicable serenity... She'd seen herself as part of the whole, integral, needed and belonging.

She could lose herself in Shane. It would be so easy. The awareness scared her half to death.

"That's okay," she'd told Hilary, and the man whose nearness made her senses reel. "I'm not that easily converted. To me, whole food is still beer and a hot pretzel."

As they'd landed in New York, the three of them had agreed to meet in the evening for a round of wine tasting in Shane's suite.

While Shane investigated the conference rooms that were being prepped for the show, Audrey unpacked in the handicapped-accessible room she and Hilary were sharing.

Wheeling herself out of the bathroom and to the side of one of the low queen-size beds, Hilary yawned. "I know we've got a couple of hours before we're supposed to meet Shane, and I would love to get started on some serious shopping with you, but I feel stuffed."

Audrey glanced up from folding a pair of jeans into a low dresser drawer. "You hardly touched your lunch."

Hilary looked at her quizzically then laughed. "Not stuffed with food. I just feel...*stuffed*. Tired." She shrugged apologetically. "I think I'll have a little rest if you don't mind."

"No, of course not. You go ahead. I'll explore the hotel shops."

"Shopping for you is going to be a blast," Hilary said around another big yawn. "You're going to turn men's heads."

Audrey smiled doubtfully, but kept her opinions to herself. Jenna had insisted on footing the bill for the new clothes. Audrey had tried to insist on using her own savings for her work wardrobe, but Jenna had out-insisted her. Even Melanie had agreed.

"You have no idea how long my mother has wanted to do something like this for you," she told Audrey.

Tomorrow, Audrey and Hilary would embark on their shopping spree. For now, she watched the other woman align her knees with the bed then press her palms against the mattress.

"Do you want some help getting into bed?" Audrey took a step forward.

"Nope." With a surprising strength, given her slender limbs, Hilary pushed her body up as if getting out of a swimming pool. "Gotta get good at this," she grunted as she hauled herself onto the low bed.

The comment made Audrey aware once again that it

was Shane and not Hilary who held out hope that the surgeon would have good news.

Hilary settled herself against the pillows, picked up a book she'd set on the end table and smiled wearily. "I'm going to read myself to sleep."

"Sounds good."

It really did. A powerful fatigue made Audrey long to crawl into her own bed. The tiredness was familiar, the same washed-out-for-no-good-reason limpness she'd been experiencing for several months. That symptom, along with a chronic sore throat and swollen lymph nodes, had sent her to her doctor a couple of weeks ago.

Ignoring her body's protest, Audrey hauled herself to the bathroom to wash her face and brush her hair, which she allowed to fall in unfettered waves to the middle of her back. Her clothing was typically simple: a cap-sleeved white cotton blouse and dark button-fly jeans with a braided leather belt. She'd exchanged her work boots for clogs and added simple earrings—gold-plated Tiggers dangling from the posts.

She shook her head apologetically at her reflection. No wonder Jenna had rushed in with a wardrobe fund.

The second time she'd had cancer, she'd also had a powerful crush on Robbie Preston. The Prestons had held a summer party and invited her. At fourteen, she'd been bald for the second time since puberty, but one of the nurses at the hospital had convinced her dad to get her a wig to replace the baseball cap she'd been hiding beneath. Excited by the notion of looking and feeling like somebody else, Audrey had begged for a wig that was long and dark, nearly black, so she'd look like the last girl Robbie had dated.

She'd had a head full of daydreams and a tummy full of butterflies the night of the party as she walked the path leading from the employee cottages to the big house. The same nurse who'd suggested the wig had also given her a sweet muted-pink dress with spaghetti straps. It was a junior-prom hand-me-down from the woman's daughter, but Audrey's father had called her beautiful. Even though in reality she'd been a skinny sick kid with freckled gray-tinged skin, borrowed hair and huge hungry eyes, Audrey had felt as glamorous as a model.

Until she'd found Robbie Preston and some blond girl strolling toward the house on their way back from the stables.

Heart fluttering with an addictively delicious nervousness, Audrey hurried forward to catch up.

Robbie's hand caressed the blond girl's back, his fingers tracing small circles between the bared, tanned shoulder blades. And the girl was giggling.

Audrey hung back, darting behind a copse of trees as the couple paused to speak in laughter-punctuated murmurs. Because she couldn't hear what they were saying, she crept a bit closer, then threw caution to the wind and lifted her pink skirt. With amazing ease, considering she was out of shape following her treatments, she climbed the nearest oak tree and wrapped her arms and legs around a limb as she eavesdropped. The entire situation reminded her of her favorite movie, *Sabrina*, in which the chauffeur's daughter ended up with the rich man's son. It seemed almost prophetic.

Robbie's murmurs were the ones she most wanted to hear, so when he leaned his head close to the blonde's, Audrey crept out a bit farther on her branch to listen.

That was when her wig began to slip. Which never happened in *Sabrina*.

As if in slow motion, the cascade of dark hair slid over one brow. At first unaware of what was going on, Audrey tossed her head, believing she was merely shaking the hair from her eyes when in fact she shook the wig clear off her head. Shrieking, she grabbed for it, knowing a flare of hope when it caught briefly on a nearby branch. She reached as far as she could, but the wig eluded her desperate fingers, parachuting neatly to the ground a couple of yards from Robbie and his friend.

She might have maintained her cover had she not lost her balance and wound up hanging from the tree branch with a torn pink skirt and aching fingers that weren't going to hold her for long.

She swore way too much and used one of her favorite bad words as she slipped from her perch. She was vaguely aware of the blond girl screaming and of Robbie repeating the same curse word Audrey had used.

She really wasn't that far from the ground. In all likelihood, she could have let go and landed safely, albeit bruised. Still, it was a little thrilling when Robbie rushed to the spot below her, spoke as if she were a spooked horse and then urged her to let go of the branch.

Skeptical, but with her arms aching, she did as instructed. He caught her as if she were light as a feather and set her ever so gently onto her feet. The look in his eyes made her feel safe, so safe she almost forgot she was bald as a billiard ball until he retrieved the fallen wig, thoughtfully brushed it off and handed it to her.

Mortified, she mumbled her thanks and ran away, then cried herself to sleep that night, railing against the fates that had made her bald and sickly and a dork, while other girls got to be beautiful and sexy and cool.

The next day, she had vowed never again to try to be someone she was not.

Standing in the bathroom of her suite in the Marriott East Side hotel, Audrey looked in the mirror and ran a hand over her long, plain hair. Was this dull, serviceable image the real her?

At twenty-four, with a decent job, a nice place to live and some mild fun to be had on the weekends, she was acutely aware of a stinging dissatisfaction.

Marriage and family were out of the question. Unless she found out she was perfectly well, she wasn't going to involve anyone else in her drama.

Besides, who was going to sign up for forever with a woman who couldn't guarantee next month? Not to mention the fact—and if she ever met someone she really cared about who really cared about her, she would be obligated to mention that fact—her treatments had affected her ability to bear children.

Getting married, buying a house together, having babies and grandbabies and living happily ever after— that was someone else's fairy tale.

But there had to be something she would take with her from her experience on this planet. And something she would leave behind. It seemed to her that so far her life was a collection of sparks. Little fizzles that spit and protested any attempt to snuff them out, but never matured to an actual flame.

She needed to put more fuel on the fire, and the first order of business was to figure out what she wanted, instead of what she didn't want.

To travel, yes. But there had to be something more, some kind of change from okay to sensational.

Shane's face flashed before her eyes. Yes. Shane was more than a spark, even more than a flame. He was an inferno.

Again she studied her reflection. He'd asked her to be his assistant, but not because she was the best candidate for the job. In fact, she was sure he still had his doubts. And that stung her pride.

Suddenly she had an agenda for the next couple of hours. She might not be able to transform her life from okay to sensational in one fell swoop, but she could make a change.

She would begin with the easiest and most obvious thing: her.

Chapter Thirteen

Once she made her plan and decided to go full steam ahead, Audrey was glad she was doing it by herself.

Seated in a cushy gold swivel chair at a swank boutique-size salon on the upper east side of Manhattan, Audrey stared determinedly into yet another mirror while a handsome Latino man named Fuego lifted sections of her hair and said, "Hmm"—a lot.

"Pretty desperate, is it?" Audrey cracked, trying to lighten the moment for her own sake.

As she sat with her crystal goblet of water, she was so nervous she couldn't bring the beverage to her lips. Until now, she hadn't realized how much change scared the living daylights out of her.

It's just hair…it's just hair…

No matter what she told herself, she knew this experience was about far more than lopping off a few inches of dead cells. Fuego seemed to know, too.

"Just a cut?" His black eyes narrowed as he repeated her earlier request. "You know how lucky you are that I had a cancellation?" Dropping the hair he'd been combing, he propped a fist on his leather-clad hip.

"If I were you, Kentucky," he said in a light accent, "I would take advantage of me. I would tell me, 'Fuego, you god, you miracle worker, you famouser-than-that-*has-been*-from-the-seventies José, you do whatever you want to my head, because I trust you with my life.'"

He stood, waiting.

"Um…"

"Good! You can send me a souvenir from the Kentucky Derby when you get back home, because I like the pictures of the jockeys and the little whips. Okay, sit and don't move. And we get rid of this." He plucked the glass of plain water from her shaking fingers. "You need something a little stiffer."

Two champagne flutes later, Fuego had pried from Audrey the fact that once her hair had grown in after chemo, she'd promised her dad she would never cut it again. He also knew she was in New York to work at a wine show and that she wanted to experiment with clothes and makeup, but had no idea where to begin.

She knew that Fuego had once been fifty pounds overweight and had suffered from acne—he'd whispered the second half of his confession and swore he would deny it if she repeated the information out loud.

He put her under a heat lamp to set the color he'd

applied to highlight her hair. When he removed the silver foils and washed her out, she saw, even on the wet strands, shimmering gold-and-red lights.

"I used three colors," he told her, "one that perfectly matches your freckles. I'm that brilliant."

Resting his chin on the top of her head, he made sure their gazes connected in the mirror, then squeezed her shoulders. "You gonna be so beautiful you gonna recognize yourself for the first time in your life." Then he started cutting.

He kept her turned away from the mirror, putting a palm on her head when she tried to glance at her reflection. At times, the scissors moved so quickly the rapid-fire clicks reminded Audrey of Irish step dancers.

Fuego did not speak during the haircut, and at one point, when he used an electric razor on the back of her neck, the sound evoked memories that made Audrey feel as if her throat were closing.

When she was nine, her mother had cut her hair after it started falling out. Gently running her cool hand over Audrey's hot scalp, Gwen Griffin had used Henry's electric razor to dispense with the wispy remainder of her daughter's hair, keeping up a reassuring monologue about beautiful women around the world who wore scarves every day and about the gorgeous celebrities who had shaved their heads on purpose. She'd exclaimed over the perfect shape of Audrey's skull, and had kissed the top of her head when they were done, so Audrey would have a lipstick tattoo.

It had been a very long time since Audrey had allowed her thoughts to linger on Gwen, but for a second she was sure she could smell her mother's favorite white-ginger perfume.

Sitting in a stylist's chair in New York City, spending what would probably amount to hundreds of dollars on color and a cut that was deliberate and intended to make her better not worse, Audrey marveled that she could feel like a sad, bald kid in Kentucky. So when Fuego put a finger under her chin and raised her head, then stepped in front of her to cut the hair around her face, she kept her eyes averted and never once tried to peek.

When he finished cutting, he commanded, "Close your eyes," and she didn't protest as he put a hand on her elbow and led her to another part of the salon.

Once more, she avoided the mirror as he applied makeup to her naked features. "On the house," he said, then repeated the game of making her close her eyes while he led her back to his station so he could finish the hairstyle.

Audrey was beginning to wonder if she would be hopelessly late for dinner with Shane and Hilary when Fuego said softly, "Look up."

Audrey literally jumped in the chair.

Staring back at her was a young woman who must always have been confident, who must always have known who she was. The woman in the mirror was polished and radiant, with a crop of superthick, autumn-hued waves that exposed high cheekbones, big amber eyes lined in shimmering bronze shadow, and peach lips. Her freckles looked like a dusting of glitter that seemed just right.

Fuego bent down as they both gazed into the mirror.

"This is how I see you. Bold. Gorgeous. No more hiding behind 'the natural look,' okay?"

Audrey smiled. "Okay," she whispered, blinking away tears. Fuego had been right about her recognizing herself for the first time.

She wasn't gorgeous, not in the way of models and actresses and other conventional beauties. But she was more fully Audrey than she could remember being in her adult life. Everything stood out—her features, her hair, the lines and angles of her face.

"Want this?" Fuego dangled a long skein of auburn hair, tied with a hair band at the top. "A souvenir."

It looked like a horse's tail with a little more wave, but it held the memory of her father saying, "Don't you cut your hair ever again, Audrey girl. You let it grow and grow and grow."

That lifeless hank had been a talisman, as if a girl with hair to her waist couldn't possibly be sick.

Magical thinking. Fake guarantees. She and her daddy had gone through so much, it was a wonder they hadn't burned sage or bought rabbits' feet.

She smiled at Fuego and at her hair. "No, I don't want it. Maybe we could donate it. To Wigs For Kids or something like that."

"Yep. I know just where to send it." He nodded with approval. "You need clothes, girlfriend. Three doors down. Walk all the way to the back where they keep the sale stuff. And tell them I sent you."

Audrey checked her wristwatch, gasped and began fumbling her way out of the cape around her shoulders. She had fifteen minutes to get back to the hotel.

"I'll check it out tomorrow," she promised. "Right now I've got to—"

With one swift move, Fuego divested her of the cape, but he was scowling. "You are not going to demean my hair and makeup with that—" he circled his hand in front of her "—Western rural look."

"Kentucky is in the south, not the west. And I promise to buy new clothes. I was planning to shop tomorrow anyway—"

"Tonight. Three doors down." He plucked up his cell phone and pressed a button. "What's your budget? They'll have an outfit waiting."

By the time she stood in front of Shane's suite, she was an unforgivable forty minutes late, hundreds of dollars poorer and quivering with nerves. She longed to return to her room first so she could check her reflection, drop off her bag of old clothes and have a moment to get her bearings, but she hadn't taken a cell phone with her and she refused to be any more tardy than she already was. He was probably ready to fire her.

She had, however, stopped at the hotel gift shop for an apology present then got on the elevator and came straight up to the room where she was supposed to meet Shane and Hilary for wine tasting and discussion prior to dinner in the hotel's formal dining room.

She knocked on the door, her mea culpa hovering on her lips. When the door swung open, however, Shane began talking first.

"There you are! I was worried—" He stopped abruptly, and neither of them spoke.

Audrey was breathless. He looked unbelievably handsome in a perfect deep-blue suit and a shirt in a lighter hue that matched his eyes. He'd been frowning, seeming more concerned than angry when he'd first opened the door, but now he looked at her with equal parts shock, wonder and bemusement.

"Very definitely worth the wait, Miss Griffin," he murmured after several seconds had elapsed. Then he stepped away from the door and gestured her inside.

She remembered to keep her head up and shoulders back as she moved past him, the sheer skirt of her sundress lapping at her knees.

The marvelous scents of soap, cologne and Shane teased her, and she made a mental note to add perfume to tomorrow's shopping list.

A single queen-size bed, crisply made, occupied the middle of his suite. Near the window, a round table was covered with wine bottles, glasses and Cambria Estates brochures.

"Where's Hilary?"

"Migraine. She's been getting them this past year. I'm glad you came straight here. A dark room and undisturbed rest seem to help the most. I'd have called you, in fact, but I haven't got your cell number. You'll need to give that to me."

Then he muttered an Aussie curse she didn't recognize. "No one will pay attention to the wine."

Pleasure filled her.

All through the salon visit and while she was trying on her new dress, Audrey told herself she was having the makeover for her, that she was sloughing off her old life and some of her old ideas. With Shane's gaze on her and his approving words, she knew she had changed for him, too. For this feeling.

Moving as casually as she could, she perused the table set with wines. "I'm late to class."

"If you're a quick study, we'll still make our dinner reservations."

She thought this over. Leave a private suite in favor of a full dining room? "Actually, I require a lot of repetition to fully assimilate subject matter."

He raised a brow at that. "Should I cancel the reservations?"

Running her fingertip down one of the glasses, Audrey tried her hand at an enigmatic smile. "You might want to push them back a bit."

She'd captured his attention, and a tingly thrill ricocheted up and down her spine. She had a feeling she was playing with fire tonight. She certainly hoped so.

Digging through the bags she'd brought with her, she found the rectangular blue-and-gold box she'd picked up in the gift shop.

"On the plane today, you told me how you feel about wine and about Cambria, and you were so passionate about it," she ventured. "I got this for you because…I wanted to give you something I'm passionate about." She held out the box.

"Chocolate," he said, taking the gift and perusing the packaging. "Expensive chocolate."

She nodded. "Three different kinds. White to go with a Chardonnay or the rosé you talked about. And seventy-five percent dark chocolate truffles to accompany a Merlot."

"You thought this through. What's the third kind?"

"Milk-chocolate-covered honeycomb."

"What do you suggest we drink with that?"

"Milk. It would be terrible with wine, but it's my absolute favorite candy. I'm hoping you'll share."

"You're full of surprises tonight, Miss Griffin." Deep masculine lines edged his sparkling white grin. It took her breath away. Behind the swirls of her filmy gold skirt, her knees turned to jelly.

She grinned back at him. "You ain't seen nothin' yet," she murmured in a low, sultry voice she didn't know she possessed, then turned toward the table set with glasses and wine bottles. "Shall we get started?"

Who the devil was this?

Shane brought his box of handmade chocolates to the table and set it down. Audrey was studying the Cambria wines he'd placed around the table, picking up bottles, reading the labels and fingering the wine rings around the stems of the glasses. Her serene Princess Grace glide across the room was belied by the caged-animal energy he found so fascinating. He'd never met anyone less serene than Audrey Griffin. She was a tigress, not a lamb.

Her body, broad and strong in her jeans and buttoned-up shirts, was now a tall, gorgeous goddess's figure. The gold dress was tied in a halter around her neck and plunged to a V between breasts it should be a felony to cover in boxy blouses. There were women, he knew, who would lament the lush sway of hip to which her dress was currently molding. He said a mental thank-you to whoever had convinced her to flaunt her curves.

"Our blue-ribbon Chardonnay," he murmured, moving to stand only a few inches away as she studied a bottle. "We can begin there."

She handed him the bottle. Their fingers did not touch, but he noticed that her nails were still short and unpolished and that her hands appeared strong enough to hammer nails into a hoof.

Deftly uncorking the chilled bottle of Chardonnay, he poured two fingers' worth into each of two wine goblets and handed Audrey hers. When his heart began to reverberate against his ribs, he realized how much he wanted her not merely to taste the wine, but to appreciate it.

He kept his eyes on her hands and the way the practical, large-boned fingers held the stem of the glass.

Before she'd shown up this evening, his plan had been to determine exactly how much wine-tasting experience she possessed. Watching her study the color and sediment in the glass, he realized she was more adept than he'd assumed.

"I've changed my mind." He plucked the glass from her resisting fingers. "Let go."

"What are you doing? Starting with the Chardonnay is fine."

He shook his head, setting both of their glasses on the table and pulling over the chair he'd moved earlier. "Sit," he instructed, placing his hands on her shoulders and pressing her gently down.

Enjoying the bemused, off-kilter expression on her expertly made-up face, he glanced around the room, muttering, "We need something…" He looked down at her. "You don't have a scarf in one of those bags?"

"No."

"Hmm." For a moment he wasn't sure what to do. Then, reaching up to his necktie, he smiled as he first loosened then untied the knot.

Audrey's eyes narrowed suspiciously. "Isn't there a dress code at the restaurant?"

"We're going to do this blindfolded."

He pulled the tie from around his neck.

"Uh, excuse me." She held up a hand, a little interested and a lot wary. "I did take a wine appreciation course, but not once do I recall being tied up."

"I'm not tying you up—I'm blindfolding you. Big difference there." As her cheeks and neck reddened, he grinned, wondering if her frequent blushes extended all the way down her body. "Blind taste tests are one of the best ways to refine your palate."

"Go ahead then. But someday when my diaries are published you are going to have some explaining to do."

He crossed behind her. "You keep a diary?"

"I will now."

Laughing, he reached over the top of her head with the tie. "Ready?"

"Yeah, but if you expect me to use neckties to blindfold the people who come to your booth, think again. I'm not that kind of girl."

"I'll buy a few scarves."

He heard the swift intake of her breath. "You are surprisingly kinky."

Chapter Fourteen

If anyone had told Audrey a week ago that she'd be sitting still in Shane Preston's hotel suite while he covered her eyes with a necktie, she'd have bust a gut laughing. As the cool silk fell into place, however, she felt perfectly safe, infinitely curious and probably more excited than she should be.

"Wine tasting uses four of the five senses. Smell, taste, touch and sight." Shane's smooth voice both piqued her interest and lulled her. A cork creaked as he opened a new bottle. "Growing up next to Cambria, I've been tasting wine since my teens. It wasn't until last year, though, that I came to fully appreciate the truth about wine."

"Truth?" Audrey echoed.

She listened to the soft suction of the cork being extracted form the bottle and the gentle glug-glug-glug as the liquid flowed into a glass. By blindfolding her, Audrey realized, Shane had added the fifth sense, sound, to the experience of wine tasting.

"Perhaps it's too simple to say that wine is a metaphor for life," he mused, "but I believe that's true. The differences among varietals and bottled wines themselves can be subtle or striking. Certainly wine appeals to the intellect as we manipulate grapes and processes to create those differences. But in the end, it's all a mystery. Earth and weather and human contribution make a wine light or heavy, white or red, sweet or acidic. In a single wine, one might identify vanilla and butter, chalk or leather, or even a tarry scent. And it's all good."

He opened still another bottle as he spoke. Without the benefit of sight, Audrey used her nose in an attempt to distinguish between white and red, sweet and dry.

Shane reached for her hand, causing her pulse to jump. With his warm fingers curling into her palm, he guided her to the first glass. Remembering what she could from her wine course, Audrey raised the glass so that her nose was over the rim. She swirled the goblet to release the wine's aroma.

"Just the wrist, not the entire arm," Shane instructed calmly, placing his hand over hers and guiding her. "It takes practice. Never rush.

"Scent," he murmured. "The first sense to come alive when you taste blind." He gave her a few moments. "What do you smell?"

Audrey had taken the course in wine appreciation

simply for something different to do. She'd never been much of a wine drinker, before or after, but she had a good nose; her instructor had actually been impressed with her ability to sniff out nuances. Glad suddenly that she was blindfolded, she concentrated on the wine for the moment instead of the man. It wasn't easy.

She sniffed again, frustrated that she couldn't make out much. "It's…fruity," she offered, knowing that was a lackluster and painfully inexperienced appraisal.

"Try again." Fortunately she detected a note of humor in Shane's tone. "Focus. Keep your mouth open when you inhale."

Determined to say something impressive and hopefully accurate, Audrey parted her lips as instructed. She swirled her glass, inhaled, paused and inhaled again. Keeping her mouth open definitely helped.

She wished she could see the wine's color and preferably the bottle label as well in order to hedge her bets, but she felt somewhat confident when she ventured, "Apples. I smell apples. But something else, too. Peach maybe. And something flowery. Rose?"

There was a considerable silence, during which she worried that she had just made a horse's ass of herself. Then she heard the deep voice. "Taste."

No point in doubting herself now. If he thought she was a dufus, he could send her home and hire someone in New York. At least she'd come away with a decent hairstyle.

For her first sip, she rolled the wine over her tongue and remembered to exhale slightly on the swallow so that her taste buds and sense of smell could work together. The wine was too light to be a deep red. On the second sip, she moved her jaws as if she were chewing. This time when she swallowed, she felt more sure of herself and began to remember why she had liked her wine class so well.

"I taste cantaloupe. And the bouquet is almost... metallic. Not in a bad way, but I bet the wine has a high level of acid."

He didn't tell her whether she was right or wrong, which annoyed her a little, but she realized he was going to make her work for her keep.

"Color?" was all he said.

"White."

"You're sure? Not rose?"

"No. But don't ask me what varietals." Then she decided to go out on a limb. "Not Chardonnay, because the brochure Hilary gave me said that Cambria Chardonnay has butter, vanilla and oak, and I didn't get any of that this time."

Again he withheld either praise or correction. Instead, he took the glass from her hand and replaced it with another, so they could begin again. Through three more wines, he coached and she tasted, describing the aromas, bouquets and flavors and guessing at the color and varietals when she could. With each glass, her confidence grew, though he said little to encourage her. By the fifth wine, she was tasting more for her own pleasure than to please him.

She sniffed and tasted, savoring the sip. "That—is—good!"

He chuckled. "And that is the response we want in

living and dining rooms around the world. However, since we'll be entertaining questions from professional wine tasters at the booth, I'll have to ask you to be a bit more specific."

Audrey repeated the process of sniffing and "chewing."

"Mmm. It's wonderful. I may never go back to diet cola." Feeling him stiffen beside her, she grinned beneath the blindfold. He could be such a snob. "Teasing. Okay, it's heavy and peppery. Definitely red. I taste berries—maybe a blackberry or boysenberry? And there's a spice—" she sniffed again "—cinnamon! It's just brilliant. I love it."

"Grape varietal?"

"I have no idea. I've never had anything like it."

She was about to take another sip when she felt Shane move behind her to untie his makeshift blindfold. She blinked even though the lighting in the room was fairly subtle. He pulled up a chair to sit directly before her.

"You're good. Better than good. One class, no formal wine tasting since then, and yet you nailed the aromas and flavors."

"I couldn't tell you the varietals. Except on the Chardonnay."

"You'll learn. Are you sure you haven't been a closet connoisseur for years?"

His eyes were smoky, admiring, and they were filled with a warmth that rivaled the wine.

Yes, she had been a closet connoisseur—of life. Of all the things she'd read about and studied in her classes, planned for and dreamed of, but never actually participated in. She'd been a collector and critic of moments that belonged to other people, moments she'd convinced herself she couldn't, shouldn't or would not ever have.

Sadness welled inside her. She wanted to be a connoisseur. She wanted to taste the world, study each nuance, imprint all the myriad details of a rich life on her heart and in her soul.

She wanted to begin now, before it was too late.

"This wine." She raised the glass between them. "What is it?"

"Shiraz. In the States, it's better known as Syrah. I intend for it to be our signature wine. It's been my pet project for the past year."

"Shiraz." Audrey repeated the name. "It sounds like magic."

Magic was exactly what she needed. Nearly every time she glanced at Shane this evening, he was looking at her, too. What did she have to lose by going after what she wanted? And what she wanted tonight was excitement. Passion and mystery and fireworks.

She wanted to soar through the night for one glorious instant and burst into a shower of glittering sparks and then… What?

Fall back to earth, she decided. Fall back to earth as all fireworks eventually do and gracefully, willingly, fade away…

Shane, she knew, would never characterize himself as a firecracker. He had no plans to fade. Someday he would be someone's hearth fire, a steady, reliable glow. But not hers. She had no illusions about that. Well, no lasting illusions. Their disparate agendas didn't have to be a problem as long as they both knew what they were getting into.

"New York, Boston and Montreal." She gave him a small smile. "All in the space of two weeks. I can't believe I almost passed up this opportunity."

"I'm glad you didn't." Audrey began to feel bubbles of anticipation until he added, "You've got a nose for wine. You're going to do great."

"I want to learn as much as I can." She raised the glass of Shiraz to the light, studying the inky rich color. "I'm here for the adventure, though, too. The days off will be wonderful. Hilary and I talked about taking in a play tomorrow night." She looked at him from beneath eyelashes made long and thick by three coats of expensive mascara. "Do you like the theater?"

He began to nod then checked himself. "I plan to get a head start on networking. The hotel should be crawling with vintners by tomorrow night."

"Oh. That sounds exciting. But have you ever been to a Broadway play?"

"No."

"Come with us then."

Temptation flashed through his eyes, but he shook his head and stood abruptly. "I'm here to work."

Audrey rose also. "What is it about you and the F word?" His brows spiked, and she shook her head and grinned. "Fun. Are you allergic to it? Does it violate a moral code?"

His hands rested on lean, perfectly masculine hips. "It violates my work ethic. There's too much to do—"

"I bet you've never been to the top of the Empire

State Building or walked through the Metropolitan Museum of Art. I'm right, aren't I? But how can you live your whole life without seeing those things? Especially when they're practically right in front of you?"

"There's a time and a place—"

"Yeah, and you're in it. The right time, the right place. It's all here."

"This is New York. Neither the Empire State Building nor the Metropolitan Museum of Art is going anywhere. Perhaps I'll come back for a vacation—"

"It won't be the same. Another moment might come, but you'll never capture this one again. And there are no guarantees. Snooze and you could lose."

"What's special about this moment?" His voice was soft and probing. "Why should I ignore the reasons that brought me here to begin with?"

Audrey's mouth went dry. *Me. I'm here. I'm this moment.* Aloud she said, "You don't have to ignore your work. You could rewrite the agenda a little."

He cocked his head. The corner of his lips twitched.

"We could have a picnic in Central Park tomorrow. Then you could come back here, network and still meet Hilary and me for the show." When he appeared to be considering her plan, she added, "And, of course, there's tonight."

"Tonight? We have dinner reservations—"

"In the hotel. I know. That sounds nice, but I've never been to Times Square. I bet there's a real New York deli or maybe even a Polish dog stand near there."

"The special in the hotel dining room is Chilean sea bass with wasabi beurre blanc."

"Do you know there's a five-story Toys 'R' Us in the Times Square district? I read about it in my Triple-A guide."

"The chef suggests a Riesling with the sea bass. Riesling has an herbaceous note that perfectly balances the fruit. It's brilliant with seafood."

"Mmm. The Toys 'R' Us has an indoor Ferris wheel."

Audrey was still picking candy-crusted pecans out of her bag of caramel corn when she and Shane arrived back at the hotel. It was close to midnight, and though she'd yawned twice in the elevator on the way up to their floor, she was still animated and intent on her after-dinner treat.

"Ooh, I got another one." She held up a crunchy pecan. "You want it?"

Shane loved her animation, her enthusiasm for everything they'd seen, done, tasted tonight. He hadn't missed his sea bass, hadn't missed the Reisling, hadn't missed networking.

They'd eaten Polish dogs for dinner, standing up and dripping mustard and relish onto their clothes. They'd walked through Times Square so Audrey could soak up sights and sounds and smells like a sponge while he soaked up…her.

She'd bemoaned being too late to get into the New York Public Library, but had marched him along until they were staring up at the three-hundred-and-thirty foot tall Gothic spires of St. Patrick's Cathedral. Nothing bothered her, not the traffic or the crowds or the brusque manners of the vendors with whom she stopped to chat. Nothing was too small or insignificant for her to savor.

He studied the pecan she was holding. She'd offered him several, dropping them into his palm. This was the first time she'd held a nut up to his mouth, as if she planned on feeding it to him.

She hadn't been overtly flirtatious this evening, but he guessed that wasn't her way. Rather, he'd caught her in a lingering glance, a smile that lasted a few extra beats, a touch.

The moment she'd spied the Ferris Wheel at Toys "R" Us, she'd grabbed his hand. His heart had beat like a teenage boy's.

Twice he'd flirted back, wiping a smudge of mustard off her mouth with the tip of his finger; hanging on to her hand when she would have let go. It was gentle, whimsical flirting, hardly a prelude to falling into bed.

Yet here in the hallway outside their rooms, all he could think about was her, in his suite. In his bed.

She waved the pecan back and forth like a pendulum. "What do you say? One last sugar-coated pecan for the road? Come on," she teased, "you know you covet my junk food."

Her eyes were alive with laughter and playfulness. The shape of her mouth was mesmerizing when she smiled.

"Do not," he denied. "Your eating habits are abominable. I treat my body as a temple."

She lowered the hand holding the pecan and sent her gaze on a lazy trip down his body and back up again. When she returned to his face, her lips spread into that beguiling crescent-shaped grin.

"I suppose your next line is going to be something about all the girls worshipping at your temple?"

The talk of worshipping must have been getting to him, Shane rationalized, because he felt the distinct need to pray for sanity. Mere days ago, he'd known that Audrey Griffin was the antithesis of everything he needed in a woman. Tonight, she was exactly what he wanted.

"What girls?" he murmured, his voice unintentionally hushed in the quiet hotel hallway.

"The ones who think you're a god."

"No girls think that."

"Well." Her voice dropped to a barely detectable whisper. "Then some people have no taste at all."

She was staring at his mouth. And he was staring at hers.

In the next heartbeat they were in each other's arms. Shane had no idea what happened to the pecan, but he thought Audrey's mouth was the sweetest taste in the world.

Her lips parted at the merest encouragement of his tongue. He took advantage, gently licking, swirling his tongue around hers, testing and savoring her as if she were wine.

The satisfaction in tasting Audrey was so much greater than in tasting wine. Wine didn't taste back, but Audrey was equally intent on exploring him. Their arms wound around each other's backs. Their kiss deepened, and their bodies melted together like two candles softened by the flames.

If she were a variety of wine, he'd order her by the case, and he suspected he would find something new and distinct every time he tried her.

Holy heaven, he had to stop this before they got in over their heads. Slowly, carefully, he pulled away.

Audrey was breathing hard, her face flushed. He loved that, with or without her new makeup, she looked like autumn in Kentucky. Amber eyes, auburn hair; even her freckles were the color of turning leaves.

He had promised himself that his next relationship would be the real deal.

Regaining control with great effort, he said, "I'm sorry. This isn't what I intended. The evening's gone a bit differently... I hadn't planned—"

She placed her fingers across his lips. "Does everything have to be logical with you?" She inhaled quickly. "Never mind. Don't answer that. What if I told you I planned this? That there's nothing spontaneous about it?" Her gaze bore bravely into his. She didn't even blink. "The moment I walked into your suite tonight, I intended to come back. And to stay. So invite me in again, Shane. Or you'll mess up the most well-thought-out night of my life."

Everyone who knew Shane Preston knew he was a sucker for a good plan.

Groaning, he crushed her to him and kissed her once more, this time with no thought of self-control. Or of stopping.

No thought whatsoever.

Chapter Fifteen

Audrey had lied. She hadn't planned to sleep with Shane Preston on their first night in New York.

She hadn't even planned to come back to his room after their night on the town.

Shane was one more example of how unpredictable her life could be. But in this case, ohhh what a wonderful thing that unpredictability was.

At this moment, one of his arms rested beneath her head. His other arm wound around her bare waist, with his hand cupping her equally naked breast. Her backside was snuggled against his lap, his thighs warm and wonderfully hair-roughened beneath hers.

The sex had been forceful and intense, with them both straining to get as much of each other as they could, as quickly as they could. After making love, he'd moved down her body, kissing her breasts and her belly before moving back up to her lips. She'd hoped they wouldn't have to talk, and they hadn't as he'd gently and protectively turned her over, pulled her toward him and snuggled her, presumably to sleep.

His breathing was quiet and rhythmic now, but she had yet to close her eyes. She didn't plan to. Her body felt replete and more perfectly relaxed than it had in…probably forever.

She had been lying here, telling herself she had made love before, that it was not so very different with Shane. The memory of every deep, thirsty kiss and each long, hungry thrust called her a liar. If she had never had sex before, if she never had it again, at least now she knew what passion was.

Her only question was how to get out of bed, pick up her clothes and race to the bathroom without his seeing her naked. He hadn't noticed her scars yet. She'd flicked off the light seconds after he'd flicked it on. If he minded, he hadn't said.

Ordinarily, the scars she carried from her two surgeries—one to remove lymph nodes and one to remove her spleen—were battle scars she refused to hide. They were part of her and could be accepted or not. She was always willing to cut her losses if someone had a problem with her.

With Shane, however, she felt vulnerable and connected in a brand-new way. She felt as if there was something to lose. She didn't want him to know all of her. Not yet. How weird that she could be at once more intimate and less authentic with him. She needed to retreat and regroup.

Carefully, she began to remove his arm from around her. Her eyes had already adjusted to the dark, so if she could find all her clothes and tiptoe to the bathroom—

"Not a chance."

Like a band of steel, his arm dropped from her breasts to her waist and held firm.

"You're not planning to leave?" His voice was husky and possessive, roughened by sleep and desire.

"It's late. And you're tired."

"Think so?" Rolling her beneath him, Shane rose above her, easily bracing himself with his palms on the mattress on either side of her head. His legs tangled with hers, his pelvis pressing against hers.

"You wake up fast," she breathed, gasping involuntarily as he very deliberately slid both his knees between hers and spread her legs.

"Uh-huh," he murmured as he lowered his body, resting one elbow on the bed and reaching for her with his free hand.

For a man who liked to discuss and plan, he had remarkably little to say as he delved into the folds of her body, his un-shy fingers finding the most sensitive part of her and stroking until her hips lunged upward. Holding her body still with a firm leg, he touched her intimately. His tongue mimicked the movement of his fingers as his open mouth caught her moan.

Audrey grabbed at the sheets, grabbed his arms, grabbed his shoulders. Just when she thought she might explode, he pulled away, released her mouth and then covered her quivering body with his. With one hungry thrust he joined them, driving into her until he was the only thought in her head. Her breath entered in gasps and released in groans. Putting his hands under her bottom, he rose to his knees and continued thrusting, pushing their bodies to the top of a sexual cliff where they teetered a second and then fell, one right after the other, and she wanted nothing more than to make the exhilaration and closeness and perfect peace of the moment go on forever.

Shane decided he was having either a stroke or a spiritual awakening.

In the aftermath of making love to Audrey, he saw stars and felt a peculiar lightness, as if he were having an out-of-body experience.

He'd made love to her the first time because she'd wanted it, and he hadn't been able to stop himself. He'd made love to her the second time, because being inside her felt like being home and because giving her pleasure, watching her become the natural, wild creature she was in his arms, gave him a sense of pleasure and even, oddly enough, of accomplishment unlike any he had ever felt before.

"I think I'd better go to my own room."

Her words pulled him from the highly enjoyable post-lovemaking haze.

"Bad idea." He rose up on an elbow to stare down at her. There wasn't enough light coming in through the window to allow him to gauge her expression. How easy it would be to label what had happened either a mistake or a compromise. And yet, neither of those descriptions fit what he felt with Audrey in his bed.

Rolling to his left, he reached for the light. The instant it clicked on, Audrey shrieked, pulling the covers tightly around her.

"Turn it off!" she ordered, then added, "please," as if a failure to be polite was the only odd thing about her request.

Shane frowned at her in consternation. She hadn't wanted the light on when they were getting undressed, either, or when they were finding their way to the bed or making love.

He settled back against the headboard, folding his arms as he studied her, voluptuous and glorious and hiding beneath the covers. "You're not going to tell me you're shy, are you?"

She nodded furiously. "Yes, I am. Horribly. Social anxiety, you know? Please turn off the light, so I can get my clothes and get back to my room before Hilary suspects something."

Having no intention of doing as she asked, Shane smiled compassionately. "I suspected you were bashful. You're so timid in bed."

Her mouth opened soundlessly then slammed closed.

He decided not to let her off the hook. "There's medication for these anxious conditions. I'm sure if you contact your doctor—"

The pillow she hurled at his head muffled the rest of the sentence. As the bed had lots of pillows, she reached for another and prepared to throw that one, too.

Laughing, he held up his hands. "I'm kidding."

Grabbing the pillow she currently held, he tossed it aside and pinned her to the bed, staring down at her with mere inches between their faces. "The sex was great. Phenomenal. Amazing." He kissed the stubborn pout of her mouth and murmured, "Didn't you think so?"

When she tried to slink farther beneath the covers, he realized he wanted an answer. "Audrey. At the risk of sounding like a cliché, was it good for you?" He'd never needed to ask before, and suddenly his heart pounded rather unpleasantly. "Break it to me gently. Am I the only one who thought we set off fireworks?"

After only a moment, she shook her head. Her voice was low when she answered, "I saw a bottle rocket, or two. Or three."

He grinned. "A few pathetic bottle rockets? We'll need more practice." Eliciting only a weak smile, he got down to the heart of things. "Tell me about the lights-out policy. What's with that?" He glanced down at the sheet and blanket she clutched in a death grip. Slowly he reached toward the knot of her clenched fingers. "Exactly what is under there that you don't want me to see?"

Audrey set her jaw, feeling stubborn and pushed beyond her boundaries. She was sure she didn't care whether he saw her body in full light; she'd long ago come to peace with imperfection.

The problem was that, knowing Shane, he wouldn't merely peek beneath the covers; he would look inside her. He would ask questions. When he got the answers, he would look at her differently, see her as fragile. Or damaged. It was inevitable. The last thing she desired, the very, very, very, very last thing was for him to feel pity or guilt.

Above her, Shane narrowed his eyes. "This isn't going to be some strange M. Butterfly revelation, is it?"

"M. Butterfly?"

He kissed the tip of her nose. "Gentleman discovers that his beautiful female paramour is actually a man."

"Oh, yeah. Wasn't that a play?"

"It was based on a true story. Scared the devil out of every man between twelve and ninety."

"Didn't the paramour in that case have male equipment?"

"Could be."

"I think you can rest assured."

Shane grinned. "All right then, Audrey Griffin, what secrets are you hiding?" With maddening sensuality, he nibbled from her chin down her neck to the base of her throat. "You may as well show me now. I'm going to see everything eventually. You'll feel better if you get it over with."

"I will not feel better. And who says you're going to see everything? This could be a one-night stand."

Ceasing his kisses for the moment, Shane sat up, not conscious of taking most of the sheet and blanket with him. When Audrey grabbed it back to make sure she was adequately covered, his frown deepened.

"This is not going to be a one-night stand. Is that clear?"

She wiggled up against the headboard. "We could renegotiate for two."

He got right into her face. "Wrong again. That may

be the kind of arrangement you've had in the past, but that's not my style."

He looked magnificent, Audrey thought. Like a lion arching his neck, prepared to roar, his golden mane flying proudly. And she loved the way his Australian accent wrapped around the assertion, "that's not my style."

"There haven't been that many others, Shane," she told him with some humor. "And I was teasing about the one-night stand. Although you're not going to be in the U.S. indefinitely. So truthfully, whatever your style has been up to now, we know we're not forever. Right?"

Shane didn't seem to appreciate her commitment to truth in advertising. Disgruntled, he joined her in sitting with his back against the headboard. "This is a very poor form of foreplay."

"Foreplay? I think we're done for tonight."

He looked as if he would disagree, then shrugged. "After-play then. It's not going to make my top-ten list of favorite post-sex conversations, either."

"Sorry." Humor edged her voice. Suddenly she knew he was right about one thing: she couldn't hide her body from him forever. His expression was bemused, frustrated and, when she had the courage to look beyond her own pain and fear, she saw clearly that he was hurt.

He wasn't the type of man to take a woman to bed, particularly a woman who was working for him, and to ignore the emotional ramifications…even if the woman was willing to. He had far too much integrity to divorce his actions from their consequences. She had gotten involved with a truly decent human being.

Taking a breath, she made a new plan: Shane could

see her body, scars and all. The reasons behind the imperfections, however, would remain private.

Looking at his big, beautiful body leaning up against the headboard, she pushed the covers aside. Forcing herself to lie still, she let him get a good look at the pale scar that ran vertically along her abdomen and at the more minor evidence of past medical procedures on her chest. Her short hair exposed the thin faded line that ran from behind her ear to her collarbone.

He didn't hide his surprise or his curiosity or his compassion. "These are what bothered you?"

Gently he ran a fingertip along one of the marks on her chest. A shiver ran through her. A good shiver. No one had ever touched one of her scars quite that way before—like a lover. She'd never touched one with that much care.

"These are nothing." The smile she was beginning to know well—lips relaxed, one side higher than the other—touched his mouth. "I have a birthmark the same shape as the Isle of Crete. Now that's something to be self-conscious about. In fact, I can barely bring myself to swim in public."

He trailed his fingertips with a feather touch down to her belly, tickling her. She giggled. Her moods changed so quickly when she was with him.

"I don't believe you." Her gaze caressed his shoulders, chest and stomach. "I don't see so much as a freckle."

Sitting up straight, he lowered the sheet across his lap, bit by bit, until he was bared to his calves. It was the first time she'd seen all of him, every inch. And there were…oh my goodness…so many inches.

"You're looking in the wrong place."

Her gaze flew to his face. Grinning, he tapped his thigh. She glanced down again and saw the birthmark in question.

"It does look like an island."

"I'm very self-conscious about it."

She shook her head. "It's handsome."

"Thank you." He rolled over her, applying his lips to a thorough inspection of each mark. "You're gorgeous," he growled between licks and kisses and bites. Just as she thought she might not make it back to her own room at all this night, he murmured, "Where did the scars come from?"

He may as well have poured a bucket of ice water on her previously burning body. Audrey wriggled away from him, wrapping herself in the sheet and blanket and this time struggling to rise from the bed without tripping herself.

Shane watched her with desire and with regret, because he'd made her uncomfortable, when the opposite had been his intention. He simply wanted to know everything about her, this enigmatic, changeable woman for whom his hunger had not even begun to be sated.

She wasn't ready to tell him about the scars and that was fine. For now. How she got them was immaterial to their relationship. That she didn't trust him enough to tell him was material, but he would deal with that in time. Though he'd never been much of a horseman himself, he knew from watching his brother and father at Lochlain Stables that a skittish filly could not be forced into compliance. Rather, a horse like that often required an intricate dance to get to the winner's circle.

"I'm going to take a quick shower before I go." Audrey said something more, about not wanting to worry Hilary, but she mumbled most of the rest of her excuse for leaving.

He understood that he had no say in the matter. Very quickly and with a calm sense of acceptance that surprised him, he decided to let Audrey do whatever she had to do tonight to make herself more comfortable.

When Audrey emerged from the bathroom, wrapped in a towel to retrieve her clothes, she found the light nearest the bed dimmed and her lover lying on his back with his eyes closed, his breathing rhythmic and deep. Shane didn't stir a bit as she found her clothes and got dressed then quietly gathered the bags she'd brought with her.

There were no protests and no more kisses to accompany her to the door. There was nothing at all, in fact, to remind her that she had just spent the most wonderfully sensuous night of her life.

Except for the fact that the gorgeous, perfectly sculpted male lying atop the covers was buck naked.

Chapter Sixteen

The schedule for their first full day in New York was packed with activity. For Hilary and Audrey, there would be a morning of shopping and sightseeing, followed by lunch in the Russian Tea Room. Shane's morning would be spent prepping for the wine show that would begin much later in the afternoon and continue the next day. He planned to have a quick noontime meal at the hotel and meet the women afterward, since the hours immediately following lunch were reserved for Hilary's visit to the surgeon.

Hilary had been fast asleep when Audrey tiptoed into their suite the night before. This morning, she'd offered a yawning apology for abandoning her new friend and said she hoped Shane hadn't harped about wine all night long.

Having no idea how Shane wanted to handle their...tryst, Audrey had said as little as possible.

Shane met them for breakfast, helping them to the table and bending to whisper in Audrey's ear, "Sleep well?" His warm breath sent shivers down her arms.

"Like a baby," she fibbed. She'd tossed and turned half the night thinking about him. About them. "You?"

"I tossed and turned," he admitted, taking his seat. His gaze never strayed from hers. "I kept thinking of the tempting morsels at breakfast. I believe I may have dreamed about a certain one. Anticipation kept me up half the night."

Deciding that was way, way too suggestive in front of his cousin, who was obviously concerned about her doctor's appointment, Audrey extended her foot to give Shane a cautionary thwack on the shin. She connected with Hilary's wheelchair instead.

"Ow!" She did a lot more damage to herself than to Hilary, who barely glanced up. "Sorry."

"No worries," Hilary assured, perusing her breakfast menu.

Shane smirked, but picked up his menu without further comment.

"I slept like a log after my migraine medication kicked in," Hilary offered, still studying the breakfast selections. "In case anyone was wondering."

"Oh, of course! How thoughtless! I—"

"Sorry, Hil, I should have asked right away. How are—"

"No worries, no worries." She flapped a hand, not bothering to look up from the menu. "Such a nice hotel.

I didn't mind a bit staying in the room. Walls are a bit thin, though. I could have sworn I heard moans coming from your room, Shane." She set her menu aside. "I'm having Belgian waffles. With strawberries and whipped cream and a side of eggs. I'm hungry this morning."

Folding her hands on the table, she smiled at the duo that sat frozen before her. "Well, how about you two? What are you having?" Her lips stretched to an impish grin that made her eyes sparkle brightly. "You must be famished after all that…tossing and turning."

Throughout the morning, Hilary remained in a better mood than Audrey would have expected, given her upcoming appointment. She didn't say much about the turn of events, but when Audrey tried on a short dress the color of Merlot, she pointed out, "Shane would love that" and winked.

Audrey bought the dress.

Lunch in the famed Russian Tea Room excited both the women. Hilary enjoyed the day immensely and con-sistently took the lead in expressing her needs—asking for help getting into a cab, for a comfortable table at a restaurant, a dressing room to accommodate her wheel-chair. She didn't act as if she was hoping for a miracu-lous recovery at the hands of the surgeon.

Everywhere they went and in everything they did, Audrey kept up her part of the lighthearted conversation Hilary seemed to prefer today. But Shane never left her mind for long. She knew this would be a tense afternoon for him and she wanted to be present to lend support, even if she had to hover in the background.

When she and Hilary arrived at the doctor's office,

Shane was already present. He announced that he'd checked his cousin in at the front desk and that the nurse should be calling for her shortly.

Hilary's lips pursed. "Did you pick out a magazine for me, too?"

Taken aback, Shane said nothing. The snipe comprised the first truly cross words Audrey had heard from Hilary. As she wheeled herself to the front desk to check in again, Audrey leaned close to Shane to whisper, "It's common to take any control we can get in an out-of-control situation."

Shane winced. "I'm an idiot. I ought to know by now."

Audrey touched his arm lightly, intending for the contact to be comforting and brief, but he reached up, took her hand and held it as they sat down. She felt the contact all the way up her arm.

Hilary sat away from them, at the end of a row of chairs. She picked up a copy of *Vogue* and thumbed through it without much interest until a nurse emerged through a doorway and called her name. Setting the magazine aside, she headed through the door. Shane rose to follow, but hesitated until Hilary said without turning around, "Come on then. At least this way I won't have to give you a blow-by-blow later."

Audrey squeezed Shane's hand then let go. He gave her a small smile, took a step after Hilary then turned to ask, "Will you be all right out here?"

Audrey got the creeps in any doctor's office, but she nodded, gesturing toward the well-stocked magazine racks mounted to the walls. "I'll work on my fashion IQ."

That drew a grateful grin from Shane. "You could

teach them a few things," he told her, his gaze sweeping appreciatively over her. "I don't think we'll be too long today." Giving her a last look, he turned to follow Hilary and the nurse.

Audrey watched the wall-mounted clock tick the seconds, three-hundred-and-sixty of them, before Shane reemerged to make sure everything was still copasetic in the waiting room. He asked if she needed anything—coffee or tea or a walk outside—and left her only when he was assured that she was fine.

It took another forty-five minutes for Shane to reappear, this time preceded by a subdued Hilary. Shane's somber expression made Audrey's heart sink, and conversation stuck in her throat. You'd think she'd know what to say after a cruddy doctor visit; Lord knew she had experience with that. But she felt clueless in this moment, and the three of them left the suite and took the elevator to the ground floor without a word shared between them.

When they were settled in the cab for the trip back to the hotel, Hilary finally smiled at Audrey. "Sorry to keep you in suspense, but there's nothing much to tell. Only what I already knew." She gestured to herself. "What you see is what you get."

Shane spoke through a tightly clenched jaw. "Nichols isn't the only surgeon—"

"Oh, I knew it!" Hilary slapped the seat of the cab. "Nichols may not be the only surgeon around, but he's the last one I'm seeing. I'd love not to see another doctor ever in my life!"

Shane so obviously wanted to argue. It felt as if the

already muggy temperature rose ten degrees simply from the tension. Audrey willed him to remain silent, though when Hilary shot her a plaintive look, clearly begging support, she guiltily remained silent, reluctant to raise the topic of her own medical experiences in order to bolster Hilary.

Traffic was monstrous, and by the time they reached the hotel, they all knew the wine show had to take top priority.

Audrey changed swiftly into one of her new outfits, a wrap dress that Hilary had called boring, but which Audrey considered appropriately classic and ladylike. She applied her makeup lightly, still tentative with the shadows and blushers and liners.

When she emerged from the bathroom, she found Hilary watching an episode of *I Love Lucy* and giggling. "This is ripper! I remember my grandparents telling me she was the funniest actress ever, but I never had time to watch. This station is going to run episodes all night long."

"Is that what you're going to do then? Stay up here and watch TV?" Audrey tried not to sound disapproving, but she couldn't keep the concern out of her voice.

Hilary kept her gaze on the TV screen, but her mouth changed from smiling to pinched. "I intend to avoid Shane until he's had time to process what the surgeon said."

Audrey sat on one of the beds. "That's a funny thing to say."

"Why?"

"Aren't you the one who has to process it?" she asked gently. "I mean, I don't know exactly what you were told, but I gather it wasn't what you'd hoped to hear."

"It was exactly what I expected to hear, though."

She waved a hand dismissively. "Yes, I'd gotten my hopes up a bit, because everyone around me did. But I knew this doctor wouldn't want to operate—no one has." She turned to Audrey, looking her full in the face for the first time since leaving the doctor's office. "Shane's been dragging me to surgeons or dragging them to me for the better part of a year. It's he and my grandparents who can't stand the thought of my staying like this. I have to start accepting it. I have to start liking me again, and I can't if all I'm ever doing is trying to change. Or if the people I love most can't accept me." Her eyes sought understanding.

Pain, sharp and strong, lanced Audrey's heart. "I do understand," she said softly, willing her voice to remain even. "But I think Shane will come through. I know he will."

Hilary smiled at that, studying Audrey's face and eventually nodding. "I know he will, too. So will my grandparents. I'd like to stay out of Shane's way while he's learning to accept the truth, though. Less stressful for me." One of her beautiful grins lightened the sober discussion. "I'll be quite happy to order room service and watch *I Love Lucy* while he's coming to terms with the fact that he can't fix everything."

She turned her wheelchair so that she was facing Audrey more directly. "Let's have a proper look at you." She squinted. "You decided to wear the Queen Mother dress, hm?"

Involuntarily, Audrey glanced down. "I like it."

Hilary shrugged. "As long as Shane does. I quite like that he's going to be more preoccupied with you than with me in the coming months." She wriggled her perfect brows, good-humored dimples appearing in her cheeks.

For a few moments, Audrey felt discombobulated. Then she realized what Hilary was implying. "No," she protested quickly. "It isn't that way. I mean, we're not a couple. Not in the sense you mean—long-term. We're just…for now. While we're traveling together."

Hilary watched her a long time, the smile fading from her face. "Not from Shane's point of view."

"Has he said something?" Audrey couldn't think of a time when Shane had been alone with Hilary, except at the surgeon's.

"He doesn't have to say anything. I see the sparks, and I know my cousin."

Audrey was glad she was sitting down. "I'm sure he doesn't think…this time…I mean, he's going back to Australia, and I…"

Hilary's frown deepened with every word Audrey spoke. "You're crazy about him." But she looked concerned now. "Aren't you?"

"I…he's…very nice. And a lot of fun. But…" She shook her head. "Hilary, I told you I'm going to travel. I told him."

"Shane travels. That's not likely to change. My parents toured Europe, tasting wines."

Audrey lowered her voice, though there was no one present to overhear. "I told you about my health. I'm not getting involved with anyone right now."

Hilary arched a brow. "You already have."

"But not in that way!" Agitated, Audrey rose. She didn't like the implication that she was somehow misleading Shane. He hadn't mentioned a future before they'd hopped into bed. And she doubted he'd welcome a serious discussion now, after the stress of the afternoon and the pressure of the wine show.

"I can't believe you'd even want your cousin to get serious about someone who doesn't know if she's going to be alive next year, much less involved in a relationship." Audrey redirected her frustration toward Hilary. "If he is viewing this as a vacation fling, do you think he'll be happy that you're encouraging me to get serious about him?"

Sadness and disapproval filled Hilary's face. Her quiet, ladylike voice could have cut crystal. "Don't be insulting."

"I'm going to go downstairs. And do what I was hired to do." With all the dignity she could muster, Audrey crossed to the door. "Do you want me to give Shane a message?"

"Yeah, would you? Tell him I'm sorry that he's surrounded by women who are destined to disappoint him." She turned back toward her *I Love Lucy* marathon, but the laughter was gone.

Although Audrey had never worked a wine show before, she figured it didn't take a brain trust to know that this show was a bust.

The other booth assistants appeared to have been hired after an international model search. Who knew whether they could tell a Shiraz from a Chardonnay, and who cared? One come-hither smile and they drew wine tasters like bees to orange blossoms. When Audrey tried

winking at an elderly gentleman, he shook his head re-
provingly, grabbed his wife's hand and hustled her away.

Audrey glanced at Shane and sighed. They'd had
some visitors to their booth, but no lineups of people
waiting to taste Lochlain's brilliant rosé.

Shane had been all business, which was as it should
be, but he, too, seemed to be at a loss how to pump up
business. On a bathroom break, Audrey had walked up
and down the aisles of booths representing specific vineyards and had noticed a number of marketing tech-
niques that Shane did not employ.

Waiting for him to finish with a middle-aged couple
who were tasting a Chardonnay, she smiled politely as
they left and sidled up to him, her heart catching at the
concern etched onto his forehead.

"Are you thinking about Hilary?" she asked, the first
time that evening that either of them had mentioned her.

He passed a hand over his face. "Of course. I was
hoping she'd come downstairs, have a look around, at
least. She's got to be devastated."

"She's not, really." It wasn't the time or place for a
discussion, so Audrey made her protest short and to the
point. "She was watching *I Love Lucy* and giggling.
She said she wants to accept herself as she is. Mostly
she's concerned about the way you and her grandparents will handle the news." *And she's pissed off at me,*
Audrey thought, but omitted that information for now.

Shane looked disbelieving. "She's always been more
concerned about others than about herself." Thinking he
was going to go into deep denial, Audrey felt her spirits
plummet, especially when he added, "Probably she needs

more time. We'll take a break, let her rest for a while once we're back in Australia, and then in a few months—"

"Is it so important that she walks again?"

He looked at Audrey as if she'd spoken blasphemy. "Before the accident, she talked all the time about marriage and children."

"People in wheelchairs have families."

"How many men will take that on? How many young, healthy people can deal with the day-to-day difficulties and the limitations of her life?"

"It only takes one," she said softly. "All Hilary needs is one person who will love her without needing her to change."

Shane opened his mouth, an automatic protest about to emerge, until he caught himself. He shook his head, rubbed his brow and finally looked at her as if he were seeing her for the first time. Renewed appreciation lit his eyes. One strong, immensely comforting arm pulled her close. "All right," he murmured into her hair, making her feel wonderful and awful at the same time. "All right. Thank you."

This would have been the logical time to tell him about herself, about the limitations and uncertainties any man who got serious about her would face. But she couldn't do it.

Audrey knew two things for sure in that moment. First, as long as she and Shane were together, she wanted to help him in any way she could. She had somehow gotten involved with a very, very good man.

Second, she knew their relationship would be even shorter than she'd originally supposed. She had no intention of telling him about her health. Ever. Her parting gift to him would be ignorance, so that he would never feel obligated to stay.

Staying with her would ruin the plans he had for his life. Even if he didn't realize it, he was a Preston through and through. Prestons built dynasties and left legacies. Shane would grow grapes and babies and traditions on that vineyard in Hunter Valley; she knew it. But not with a woman whose odds of getting cancer again were better than her odds of ever getting pregnant.

She was falling in love with Shane, but their relationship would be over before the last bottle of wine was uncorked.

Cambria Estates Vineyard had a mediocre performance at the show, and Audrey's relationship with Shane didn't progress any further. Towards the end of the evening, an old friend of his stopped by the booth and invited him to a very late dinner. A strong fatigue was claiming Audrey, so she retired to her suite around ten o'clock.

Hilary was already asleep, but had left on one small light. A lone room-service tray sat on the table, the dishes neatly re-covered. A novel lay on the nightstand between the beds. The clothing Hilary had worn that day had been put away, and in the bathroom, a toothbrush, washcloth and bottle of moisturizer sat neatly to one side. She must have stayed in the room the entire evening.

Once again, Audrey felt awe and admiration. Hilary had a physically delicate appearance, but inside she was finding the steely strength to care of herself without the use of her legs.

Taking time to remove her makeup despite her exhaustion, Audrey brushed her teeth and then crept quietly into the bedroom. When she crawled between the sheets, she felt strangely chilled and utterly wiped out. Almost against her will, she reached beneath her arm to feel the lump that had sent her to her doctor a few weeks ago. It was still there, perhaps a bit larger. Perhaps the same. She couldn't be certain. She whipped her hand down to her side then reached up to turn off the light, burrowing under the covers as if she could hide from the truth.

Near shivering only seconds ago, suddenly she felt flushed. Last night she'd felt normal and whole and loved in Shane's arms.

In ten days, the wine shows would be over. Shane and Hilary would return to Australia. And she would return to a life in which denial and audacity had become her buffers against loneliness and fear.

She wanted to wait up for Shane, to knock on his door when she heard him come back to his suite. She wanted to crawl into bed beside him and let their lovemaking banish the shadows.

It might have been fatigue, or perhaps the stubborn certainty that she shouldn't get too dependent on any one person, that kept her in her bed, thinking about Shane instead of being with him. But just before she closed her eyes, she came to a decision that pleased her.

She was sure Shane's setup of the Cambria booth had been partly responsible for today's lackluster performance. But she had played a part, as well, with her holier-than-thou sensibilities and her stubborn refusal to step outside her comfort zone.

Well, starting tomorrow, she would defy her own boundaries. She would become the booth bunny he needed during the day…and the sex kitten she wanted to be at night.

Ten days, nine nights.

Suddenly it seemed all right to be sleeping alone again. She was going to need her rest.

Chapter Seventeen

They were on a plane to Boston before they had a chance to rehash the New York wine show, to evaluate what worked and what didn't.

The flight attendants had served refreshments, and Shane, Hilary and Audrey were settled comfortably for the short trip. Shane tried to downplay Cambria's lack of success, but Hilary wasn't having any of it.

"Give me figures, Shane. How many wholesalers and how many retailers said they wanted to set up accounts?"

"You know it doesn't necessarily work like that, Hil. The vendors and restaurateurs visit all the booths—"

"Okay. Which ones indicated they might call to set up accounts?"

He hesitated a second too long.

"Audrey, you tell me," Hilary requested. "Was Cambria a big bang or a tiny little fizzle?"

"Something in the middle, I think," Audrey answered, trying to be politic. She glanced at Shane, who shrugged and shook his head.

"We gave out a few business cards and took a few," he admitted. "Not nearly as many as I'd hoped."

Hilary nodded thoughtfully. "Any ideas on what happened? Other than the fact that I bailed out on you, for which I apologize." Shane began to protest, but Hilary waved off platitudes. She fished a roasted peanut from a small foil package and popped it into her mouth. "This is my responsibility, too," she said decisively. "I'm not certain it's what I want to do for the rest of my life, but it's what's in front of me, and it's my grandparents' legacy. The thing is, I've only been to a few wine exhibits. So unless there was a poor turnout, I'm not sure how to change things."

Audrey glanced at Shane, pleased by the surprise she saw in his expression. She knew that for his bond with his cousin to remain strong he had to begin to see her as strong and vital, the way she wanted to be seen, and not as a chronic patient.

"The turnout was good," he said, honoring Hilary with a calm and candid recitation of the facts. "The other booths seemed to be doing a brisk business most of the night."

Hilary winced. "Ouch. So what's the diagnosis, doctor?" Her dimples appeared as she grinned impishly. "That is not a reference to yesterday, by the way. Though I have been wondering if you phoned the grands?"

"I did."

She nodded. "Thank you. I'll call, too, when we get to Boston, and let them know I'm fine."

"All right." Shane left it at that, and Audrey felt so proud of him that she reached over and squeezed his arm.

Save for taking her hand at breakfast and whispering that he'd missed her the night before, he had gone out of his way, it seemed, not to touch her excessively or to flaunt their relationship. She was sure his reticence was in deference to Hilary, and she respected that, too.

Now, however, he held her hand, twining their limbs on the armrests between them. Shane sat between her and Hilary this time, and when she smiled up at him, she caught a glimpse of Hilary, too, eating her peanuts and smirking, well aware of the contact between her and Shane.

Audrey cleared her throat. "I have an idea about what went wrong." Both Hilary and Shane looked at her.

She couldn't tell whether Shane was pleased or merely humoring her when he held on to her hand and nodded. "Go on."

Proceeding to give them a brief overview of what she had learned in her marketing course, Audrey ventured, "If I were you, I'd emphasize the Aussie import angle. It's very glamorous these days. And I'd come up with a trademark phrase that tells people immediately who you really are—to make them remember you. I took a calligraphy class once—no cracks about the number of classes I take," she warned, "so we could work up a decent poster. Maybe use Internet access at the hotel to print out pictures of Australia. And for the future, I would definitely send a mixed case of Shiraz, Riesling and rosé along with some brochures to several Aussie celebrities—Cate Blanchett, Russell Crowe, Naomi Watts, Hugh Jackman—and ask them for quotes you can use in your advertising—ASAP."

Shane and Hilary glanced at each other. Then Shane asked, "Anything else?"

In for a penny, in for a pound. "Yes." She took a breath. "You really need a booth bunny."

Hilary gasped. Shane's brows rose enough to create a series of handsome character lines on his forehead. "Are you volunteering?"

"Yes." She smiled and looked past Shane as further inspiration struck. "Me…and a friend."

"From the land that brought you Cate Blanchett, *Moulin Rouge!* and Vegemite, may we present Australia's newest revelation—Cambria Estates Vineyard."

Hilary's sexy, accented purr poured into the aisle in front of the Cambria booth at Boston's immensely popular Mostly For Merchants wine show. Dressed in a deeply plunging gown of I-won't-be-ignored red, she flirted beautifully with the crowd, illustrating that Australia did, indeed, produce classics.

On the other side of the booth entrance, Audrey balanced a silver platter of crackers topped with caviar, graciously offering morsels to passersby. As Shane poured wine and conversed with a steady stream of patrons, he glanced at Audrey as often as he could without seeming rude to the prospective clients he was supposed to be engaging in conversation. He had an alarming urge to close the damn booth right now and take Audrey up to his suite, so he could have her to himself until morning. Morning five days from now. He had a strong suspicion that where Audrey Griffin was concerned, his appetite would remain immodest.

Tonight she was wearing a Bordeaux-colored dress that reminded him of wine and tempted him to taste her. Cupping her curves, the deceptively simple sheath ended three inches above her knees, showing off the legs he loved to look at…and loved even more when they were wrapped around him.

Damn, it hadn't been easy leaving her alone last night. If she hadn't seemed so tired, he never would have gone off with his friend while she returned to the hotel suite.

"How many varietals do you grow at Cambria, Mr. Preston?"

With effort, Shane returned his attention to the gentleman in front of him. As he conversed, however, he continued to keep an eye on the men surrounding Audrey, and there were, he noted, quite a few. Pleasure and jealousy, in unequal measures, rose within him. She was certainly entitled to the attention. She was beautiful, sexy, challenging and smart. In one short day, she had transformed herself, transformed the booth and transformed Hilary, who was alive and glowing in a way Shane had not seen since before the accident.

He wanted to thank Audrey. Now. In private. Over and over.

"How do you characterize the Cambria Shiraz?" inquired a middle-aged man who said he owned a number of seafood restaurants and was looking at new wines for his list.

Shane was focused on the bloke's face when the question was asked, but his gaze strayed again to Audrey as he answered. "Our Shiraz is as flexible as it is full-bodied. It's timeless, but I think you'll find it surprising as well. I'd characterize it as multifaceted... complex...spicy." Audrey laughed with a woman whose husband had dribbled a bit of caviar onto his chin. She said something Shane couldn't hear, but the man spewed a bit more caviar and the wife laughed harder. Grinning, Shane concluded, "One taste, and I guarantee you won't forget it."

He began making plans for after the wine show.

Later, in the privacy of a beautifully appointed suite, tangled in the bedclothes of a wonderfully soft bed, Audrey decided that the aftermath of lovemaking with Shane would remain one of her sweetest memories. And not only because the sex was great, which it had been, but because at one point Shane had risen, retrieved a double-handled paper bag from the dresser and proceeded to shower her with expensive candy he'd picked up in the hotel gift shop. Truffles had rained onto the bed.

"Look at that," Audrey pointed out now. "We got chocolate on the sheets."

Shane rolled over her, holding up a Chambord chocolate cordial he'd just bitten into. He had that look in his eye, the one that told her he wasn't nearly as respectable in bed as he was out of it. "We'll have to leave housekeeping a very—" he tilted the chocolate dome, dripping raspberry liqueur onto her right nipple "—big—" and then onto her left "—tip."

Folding her arms on the pillow behind her head, Audrey settled back and tried to look stern. "You are planning to clean that up?"

"What do you think?" Knowing how much she liked her sweets, he gave her the rest of the chocolate while he cleaned up the liqueur.

The Boston wine show was a two-day event, which did not recommence until early evening on the second day. After much discussion and a bit of good-natured disagreement about how to spend their day, Shane, Audrey and Hilary decided to take an historic walking tour of the city, trekking a section of the Freedom Trail that led them from Boston Common to Copp's Hill in North End.

By following a path formed in some places of red bricks or granite stones embedded in the sidewalk and in other places a simple painted red line, they passed one site after another that together made up one of the most historically rich locations in the United States. They took turns pushing Hilary's wheelchair up Beacon Hill to see the Massachusetts State House and the neighborhood's elite row houses, then backtracked to the Park Street Church, where Samuel Smith's "America" had had its first public performance during a Fourth of July celebration in 1832.

The mood of the three of them was light-years away from that on their second day in New York. Shane and Audrey laughed and joked and held hands freely, unless one of them was helping Hilary, who often assumed the role of tour guide, hurrying them along to the next des-

tination amid facetious comments about how difficult
it was to travel with a pair of "school kids." After a
couple of hours of sightseeing, they were ready to stop
for lunch at one of the restaurants that had indicated a
desire to add Cambria Estates wines to their list.

Hilary's obvious enjoyment the night before and
again today went a long way toward reassuring Shane.
Several times, though, Audrey caught Hilary watching
them with a troubled frown, and she knew that Shane's
cousin was concerned about him being hurt.

Audrey reassured herself by remembering that Shane
did not talk about the future with her; in their relationship, at least, he tried his hand at living firmly in the
present. Still, as the cozy trio moved around Boston, she
found herself falling into a sense of belonging with
these people, a feeling she hadn't experienced since her
dad had passed on. Perhaps even before that, because
with only the two of them, family moments had sometimes felt incomplete.

When Hilary mentioned her grandparents in passing,
Audrey wanted to know more. She asked questions
about them and about Shane's brother and parents,
soaking up the information as if she were learning about
long-lost relations. She knew darn well that she was
setting herself up, but couldn't stop herself.

By the time they made their way back to the hotel,
she was utterly exhausted and happier than she had
been in years.

The second night of the show went even better than
the first. With no letup in activity from the time they'd
awakened that morning until late in the evening, when

the last stragglers left the booth, Shane and Audrey were
bleary with fatigue. Hilary had returned to her suite an
hour earlier at Shane's insistence, but Audrey had opted
to stay so she could begin packing the items they needed
for the next show, which would happen one week later
in Montreal.

"We have a morning flight back to Kentucky," he
reminded her as he fit the last bottle of unopened wine
into a box divided with corrugated cardboard.

"Whose bright idea was that?" she inquired with a
tired jab.

"I lacked foresight," he admitted. Turning toward
her, he took her in his arms, linking his hands at the
small of her back. "If you go upstairs now and get
straight to bed, you'll have about five hours of sleep
before you have to wake up."

Surprise and disappointment brought a frown
swooping to her brow. Despite their exhaustive pace, she
had felt good, energized the whole day. But perhaps he
was tired and trying to let her know—

And then she felt it—the slow, sensuous slide of his
palm massaging her lower back. Pulling her closer, he
nuzzled her neck. His warm breath tickled her ear when
he whispered, "I'll give you my key card. You climb into
bed and when I get there I'll give you a massage to help
you relax. No funny business. You have my word."

Happiness and anticipation returned, but she kept
her voice neutral. "Let me get this straight. You want me
to come up to your room after a long, backbreaking two
days—and all you're going to do is give me a massage?
That's the reward for all my hard work and devotion?"

As she spoke, she inched her body closer, even when he started to pull back. Nearly his height in her high, stiletto heels, she pressed her thigh right where she thought it would do the most good. At his body's response, she grinned and reached up to delve her fingers possessively through his hair. "Shane Preston, I've got way more smarts than that. Now, make me an offer I can't refuse."

With a deep, satisfied chuckle, he set out to oblige. While the merchants around them packed up to go home, Shane pulled Audrey to the far end of the booth, where he cupped the back of her head in his palm and proceeded to talk to her with his lips, his teeth, his tongue. He left no doubt that he was hungry for her and that he had more than enough energy to make her miss her beauty sleep.

As soon as Shane let her up for air, Audrey caught her breath, a little awed by the display she'd provoked. Leaving no doubt about her response, she melted in his embrace, murmuring, "Well, there you go. If that was a question, the answer is *yes*."

It proved a bit more difficult for Shane and Audrey to see each other once they were back in Kentucky for the week before the Montreal event. Hilary caught a cold on the plane, a nasty bug that moved quickly into her lungs. Shane phoned Audrey several times, but between a visit to urgent care and a trip to the pharmacy, he was unable to make it out to Quest for the first couple of days.

Audrey wanted to check on Hilary, but Shane assured

her that everything would be fine, and she didn't want to intrude or to add to his pressure by making him think he had to worry about her needs, too. She was busy with her work at the stable, but missed Shane every moment of the day. Even more at night, when no amount of imagining or remembering could take the place of his actually being with her.

The negative publicity following the racing commissions' ban of Leopold's Legacy had led several owners to remove their horses. Still, others intended to remain and take advantage of Quest's reputation for spotting weaknesses and building strengths during their excellent training sessions. After being away, Audrey found herself working nonstop. She spent an afternoon and the following morning shoeing horses and was just sharing her lunch with Biding Her Time when Melanie Preston entered the stable, sweaty after a long morning of riding.

The women had seen each other the day before, but hadn't had much time to chat.

"I really do love that haircut," Melanie said, turning to lean her back against the wall next to Biding's stall. Melanie kept her own hair short, which perfectly complimented her petite frame.

Audrey held a chunk of carrot out to her favorite horse, who nibbled it greedily. "Thanks. I like it, too. Although for a minute I thought Biding here almost didn't recognize me, did you, girl?"

Melanie watched the gray filly finish the carrot and then shove her nose toward Audrey. "She's a funny horse, that one."

"What do you mean?"

"She seems to have all the ingredients of a good racer, and I think she really wants it, but…"

"What?"

Melanie shrugged. "That's just it—I don't know. I can't figure her out at all, and I know she stumped her other riders. I think she could be a push-button, but no one knows which button to push. It's as if she's waiting for the right person to trust."

An uncomfortable feeling skittered through Audrey's veins. "She needs more experience, that's all."

"With the ban in effect, she won't get it." Melanie dug the heel of her boot hard into the ground. "Damn this whole miserable mess." Running her hands through her hair, she growled. Obviously, trying to shake off anger and concern over Quest's predicament had become a full-time occupation. Melanie gestured at Biding Her Time. "Dad's thinking of selling her to Ray Bedford, so—"

"Bedford!" Audrey whirled on Melanie so fast and spoke so sharply that Biding tossed her head and retreated to the rear of her stall. "He'll race her in claiming stakes!" Horses raced in claiming stakes could have any number of owners before they were put to use as breeders. If that happened to Biding, she might never find the right combination of trainer and rider. And it was highly likely that Audrey would never see her again, never wrestle with her over a shoe, or make her trade a kiss for a carrot. Audrey wouldn't even have the comfort of knowing where the horse was. It would be like a death.

"I'm sorry." Quickly, Melanie reached out to touch Audrey's arm. "I didn't know she meant so much to you."

Audrey felt tears rush to her eyes and furiously blinked them away. The huge wash of loneliness and need shocked her, leaving her vulnerable. For the first time, the threat of the following week, when Shane would return to Australia and she would remain here, filled her chest. Like a foreign body, it crowded her lungs and made taking a complete breath impossible.

Nothing was permanent. Not a horse in a stable, not the happiness she'd been feeling. Not love. Not even her. She'd spent half her life making herself look at that truth, congratulating herself for not shrinking away, like so many people did, from plain facts. So why couldn't she breathe? Surely the sale of one horse couldn't bring her to her knees?

"She doesn't mean that much to me."

Melanie inclined her head. "Audrey—"

"She doesn't." Then, mumbling an excuse, Audrey crushed the brown paper sack that held her lunch and rushed from the stable on trembling legs.

So much of the grief she'd held at bay, so much of it, rolled through her like a wave with no shore upon which to crash. It simply built and built.

She moved as fast as she could, feeling herself beginning to perspire, feeling the mad pumping of her heart. It was crazy to be so upset. Change and loss were part of life. She knew that, had encoded it in her DNA. Yet the closer she got to her cottage, the more difficult it was to move.

Her home had been empty for over a year save for her and one giant, shaggy flea trap. She'd been handling it fine. She could still handle it.

But Shane's image rose persistently before her, until she could feel the comfortable rumble of his chest when he held her close and laughed…and she could see his blue eyes, alive with interest as he talked about his grapes…

She saw mornings when the sun wasn't yet up, but the coffee was brewed and the sheets were warm, and she and Shane sat up in bed, brainstorming ways to improve Cambria's wine sales. And they would shush each other so they wouldn't wake the kids…or the dog…keeping as quiet as they could so they might steal another rare moment alone before the whole household was awake and noisy…

Audrey was still a good twenty yards from her cottage when her trembling body gave out. She fell to her knees on the emerald grass, letting her breathing slow. There was so much she had never allowed herself to long for. So much to want in this short, beautiful life.

And that's when she realized—

Losing someone wasn't the threat. Loving them was.

Chapter Eighteen

Three large cardboard boxes were packed, sealed and ready for the thrift shop by the time Audrey paused for dinner.

Weak and tired from the emotion of the afternoon and the decision to begin packing her belongings and cleaning the cottage, she experienced more of a need to eat than a desire. Pushing up from the floor, she rubbed the small of her aching back and trudged to the kitchen, where her usual frozen dinners, cheese-stuffed crackers and cold cereal held little appeal. Her father had tried to put a hot dinner on the table most evenings, even after she'd reached an age when she surely should have fended for herself or, better yet, cooked for him.

Truthfully, Henry hadn't been much of a chef, but

at least he'd gone to the trouble of cooking up a box of pasta and putting some salad in a bowl. What an adjustment it must have been for him, having to become mother and father and nurse to his young daughter, with no transition and no warning before Gwen ran out on them.

Feeling a curl of nausea, Audrey tried to push the thought of her mother to the back of her mind. She had little success and didn't expect any, really; this seemed to be the day when the past was relentlessly determined to meet the present.

A few crackers with a smear of peanut butter would have to suffice until her appetite picked up.

The doorbell rang as she was unscrewing the lid on the peanut butter jar. Audrey turned her head, and though the door was solid wood and she could see nothing, she knew instantly who was there. And she was glad. Her limbs filled with the most energy she'd had all day.

She opened the door without asking who was there. Shane's sexy, weary smile greeted her, as she'd known it would, and she threw herself into his arms before a word was spoken. After a moment's surprise, his arms wound round her, although awkwardly so. As if from a distance, she realized he was carrying something, but once she started kissing him, she couldn't quite bring herself to stop. With blind, choppy steps, mouths hungrily seeking each other, they half walked and half stumbled into Audrey's small home. Shane guided her to the kitchen counter, where he deposited the plastic bags he'd brought in, and then she guided him down the short hallway, past the boxes she'd packed and into her bedroom. They didn't emerge until it was long, long past dinnertime.

"The food's cold." Shane spoke while toying with the inch of thick, silky hair at Audrey's nape.

Enjoying the sensation, she twirled her fingers lazily through the thatch of golden curls on his chest. Such a lovely contrast, the light hair and bronze skin. "What food?" she muttered. Falling asleep right now would be perfect.

"Chinese. Mu shu, Szechuan chicken, broccoli in black bean sauce, spring rolls. I wasn't sure what you liked, so I got a variety. Are you hungry?" His palm, warm and broad and soothing, wandered leisurely down her spine.

She closed her eyes. "Hmm. Chinese takeout. My dad and I used to have that all the time. Did you go to the little place next to the mom-and-pop video store?"

"The Twin Dragon." He kissed the top of her head, and she felt him smile against her hair. "I bought a bag of almond biscuits."

Knowing he referred to the crisp, crumbly, shortening-rich cookies she had never been able to get enough of as a kid, she snuggled against him and practically purred. "My favorite."

"I could be persuaded to let you have my share. If I'm properly compensated."

Audrey laughed. "I'm a little tired, but I'll see what I can do." She rose up to kiss him, but Shane slid his hands up her arms and held her still.

"Tell me about the scars."

For several beats, neither of them moved. Then

Audrey twisted out of his grasp and turned to rearrange the pillows. Taking time to collect her wits, she punched a pillow into a ball she tucked behind her back. Smiling falsely, she said, "That's not exactly flattering, you know. A girl tries her best moves, and all you can think about are her flaws?"

"I don't think they're flaws," he protested. "They're part of you. Part of some battle you fought, and I want to know what it was. I want to know how it affected you in here." He rested his fingers on the hollow between her full breasts, his touch not sexual, but sincere and possessive. "I want to know you."

She swallowed hard, believing him. Before he'd shown up tonight, however, she'd come to a decision about her immediate future. She knew exactly what she would be doing after Montreal, and her plans could not include one very tall and fabulous, sincere, possessive, marvelous Aussie. For his sake and for hers, tonight would be fun and memorable, but it would not include discussions that were *deep* and *meaningful*.

"If you want to know me," she said, willing him to change course, "then ask me what I liked for lunch in kindergarten. Ask me what my favorite book of all time is. My favorite movie."

With an expression that was part exasperation, part wry affection, he relented. "What did you like to eat in kindergarten?"

"Peanut butter and marmalade, hold the peanut butter."

"What's your favorite book of all time?"

"Anne of Green Gables."

"Movie?"

"*The African Queen.*"

"Where'd you get those scars?"

She swore softly. Pulling the pillow from behind her back, she threw it at him, leaping off the bed and lunging for the big T-shirt she'd been wearing when he showed up at her door. Forgoing undergarments this time, she tossed it over her head then literally hopped into her jeans.

"Last one to the Chinese food is out of luck!"

Aware that Shane left the bed and was struggling into his clothes so he could follow her, Audrey jogged through the now dark hallway and flicked on lights in the living room and kitchen.

"Ow!" A curse followed.

"What happened?" She whirled at Shane's exclamation then winced without his having to answer. The boxes. Rats. Trotting to the hall, she turned the light on there, too. "I'm so sorry. I pushed them against the wall, but this hallway is so narrow. I'll make it up to you— you can have an extra spring roll."

He wasn't listening. The boxes had commanded his attention, along with the piles of books and miscellany she'd stacked in the hall.

"Thrift store," he read the labels she'd affixed to the boxes. "Thrift store, thrift store…" Arriving at the books, he looked at the paper she'd taped to the top of the stack. "Storage." He turned to her. "Moving?"

His expression was difficult to read. Audrey spread her hands. "I told you I want to travel. Eventually the Prestons will need this cottage for another employee. I mean, if I don't come back. There's no point in leaving everything for the last minute." She smiled, tried to keep things light. "What if I'm in Madrid and decide to take a job serving tapas? Or I could be in France, learning to bake the perfect baguette. It would be a crying shame to have to drop everything and fly home just to pack some old books."

"It would indeed." He agreed quietly, but Audrey didn't like the way he was watching her, as if he thought he could find the truth by looking long enough or hard enough.

"I thought I'd make us both a plate of food and pop it in the microwave. Is that okay?"

"Fine." He walked toward her, a beautiful, looming presence in jeans and a shirt he hadn't buttoned. Catching her by surprise, he grasped her by the shoulders and lowered his mouth to hers. His seeking tongue encouraged her lips to part, deepening the kiss into something bold and demanding.

He took one hand from her shoulder and stroked it down the side of her body, his touch insistent as he cupped her bottom and pressed her firmly against him. Audrey felt her body begin to burn, desire returning so fast and so feverishly that when Shane disengaged from the kiss and let her go, it took a moment for her to come back to earth. His next words helped.

"Be sure to put me on your travel itinerary. I can't teach you how to make a baguette, but I'll show you a good time in Oz." He winked and walked around her. "I think I'll take that extra spring roll."

Audrey, energized not so long ago, felt spent and weighed down again as she followed him into the kitchen. "Dibs on the plum sauce."

* * *

Shane stayed away from Audrey the rest of the week. It wasn't easy. He wanted to be with her day and night. When he visited his aunt and uncle, he had to force himself not to ask questions about her, like whether she'd formally given her notice. It took sheer will not to visit the stables.

More than he could say, he regretted his behavior the last time they were together. Making her believe he was fine with a brief fling had left a sour taste in his mouth. Lies always did.

While Shane unpacked his suitcase, the passion and romance of Montreal mocked him from the window of his hotel suite. He and Audrey were flying solo for this show.

When it had become clear Hilary should stay in Kentucky to nurse a case of bronchitis, Jenna had insisted that she move into one of the Prestons' guest rooms. Aware that arguing with Jenna would simply kill time, he'd urged Hilary to accept. Besides, he could never have left her on her own in Kentucky; when he loved, he loved all the way. Feeling responsible for the people he cared about was simply part of life.

Fortunately, it hadn't taken long for Hilary to agree with Jenna's plan, and they'd moved her into the house yesterday. Audrey knew about it; she'd visited Hilary at the motel earlier in the week.

Hanging the last of his trousers in the closet, Shane zipped his suitcase, stowed it and walked to the window, where he stared at the eclectic city that could, he suspected, be the last place he and Audrey Griffin pursued their affair. With Hilary in Kentucky, he had assumed that he and Audrey would share a room. At the last moment, however, he'd decided not to cancel Hilary's reservation, realizing Audrey might want her privacy. And the distance.

How could he pretend to understand her needs when they were far, far different from his?

He was here in Montreal, alone with the woman who kept him up nights, and he had no need for time or space away from her. Quite the contrary. He couldn't get enough of her.

Never before in thirty-six years of life had he met someone so surprising, so unpredictable, and so utterly confounding as Audrey. Never had he expected to fall so deeply for someone who wouldn't fall for him.

Shane rubbed his hands over his forehead and through his hair. Audrey had wanted to see more of him this past week. It had been his choice to keep his distance, partly as a test to see if he could put her from his mind—he failed—and partly to make her realize she wanted him more than she thought.

Welcome to your second childhood, Shane Preston.

Catching sight of his reflection in the window, he had a strong urge to punch the glass. Unrequited love—it sucked.

The knock on his door saved him from another round of rumination about his booth assistant, and he crossed the room, hoping it was someone from housekeeping to pick up the pants he wanted pressed.

He opened the door, thinking about trouser creases, and stood face-to-face with the woman who made him think only of taking his trousers off.

Audrey had exchanged her sedate traveling suit for a filmy summer dress that seemed to repeat the colors in every strand of her red-bronze hair. With little or no makeup, her freckles showed, dusting her nose and cheeks, tiny, tiny dots the same shade as her big amber eyes. She was a breath of fresh air, a taste of autumn in the heat of summer. Like a tongue-tied teenager, he stood rooted to the threshold and stared.

With a smile as pure as the pink of her cheeks, Audrey said, "My turn to take you out on the town."

If Shane had worried that the romance of Montreal would mock him during his stay, he was wrong. Apparently Audrey had done her research, making sure they toured enough of the multicultural city to feel as if they'd traveled across a few centuries and several countries in one sensuous afternoon.

Cobblestone streets, graceful wrought iron and stained glass seemed to marry, rather than conflict, with more urban North American sensibilities in architecture. Standing side by side, Audrey and Shane gazed in awe and admiration at Place Jean-Paul Riopelle's fountain-sculpture, made famous by its ring of fire. They viewed the multiple towers of Place Ville Marie and went below the city streets to explore the underground pedestrian network—twenty miles of passages leading to stores, restaurants, hotels and even universities.

As lovers, they should have held hands while walking the character-filled city. It wasn't until Audrey took them to their dinner destination, however, a small vine-filled dining room in Montreal's Little Italy, that the distance between them evaporated.

Bunches of plastic grapes hung by the dozens from lattice woodwork around the cozy mom-and-pop restaurant. Checkered tablecloths, drippy flickering candles and sometimes-fuzzy recordings of Italian crooners transported the diners to a different time and place.

"Montreal is the second-largest French-speaking city in the world, and we're listening to Dean Martin sing 'Volare'—with static," Shane cracked, sotto voce, as they studied the hand-lettered menu.

Sitting beside him in the small booth, Audrey nudged him with her elbow. "Shh." But she had to frown over a giggle. "I have it on very good authority that Papa Giovanni makes the best gnocchi this side of the Atlantic."

"On whose authority?"

"Suki Collins."

"Does Suki Collins author travel guides?"

"No, she serves hot wings at Herman's. But she grew up in Quebec."

Shane laughed, decided on the gnocchi, closed his menu and put his arm along the back of the booth, brushing the base of Audrey's neck.

She turned toward him. "Are you trying to make a move on me?"

She spoke facetiously, but that was as close to outright flirtation as they'd gotten all day. It occurred to Shane that he was tired of resisting his own instincts. "Yes, I am."

Audrey's gracefully arched brows rose in surprise. "'Bout time," she said softly, scooting closer so that she rested neatly against his side.

The simple closeness felt so damn good that Shane

knew he would never be able to strategize in his relationship with her. He wanted her in his bed and in his life. He wanted her so badly that he would take anything he could get. Wryly shaking his head, he tried to look inside her, past the evasions and secrets she wouldn't share. "What do you want, Audrey Griffin?"

She stared back at him, satisfyingly dazed. "Gnocchi with marinara," she murmured.

Grinning crookedly, he squeezed her shoulder. "Think longer term."

Instantly, he saw her sober. "I want this weekend, Shane. I want right now." She gazed down, fiddling with her napkin before looking up again to search his face. "I told you from the beginning that's who I am. Can't that be enough?"

No. Hell, no. Settle for a weekend when a lifetime could be on the table? Why should he? Why should she?

With one look at her pleading expression, he knew there were no words to convince her, not tonight. Maybe not ever.

He looked at the nervously parted lips, as pink and soft as ever, at the eyes that had challenged and sparkled and swooned at him. His gaze dipped lower to the body he had already adored with his and at her strong, almost muscular arms. She had a bosom he could spend a lifetime admiring and the legs of a champion. But it was her busy mind and fierce heart, her outspokenness and humor that had him hooked.

Anger burned in his gut, edging perilously close to resentment. She wanted him to be someone he was not. Someone who could take pleasure without possession and divorce his mind from his actions. But he had plans, dreams for his life, and they pulsed as strongly as her need for freedom.

Her hand moved to his thigh, resting there, and though the touch was meant to be more questioning and reassuring than sexual, it set his whole leg on fire. Passion warred with principle, the battle short and bitter. Shane lowered his head for a kiss that was hard, possessive and promising. If the weekend was all she was offering, so be it; his plans and dreams were damned.

"Vous avez les plus beaux yeux au monde."

"Non, monsieur. Ce n'est pas vous qui parle. C'est le vin."

Laughter, throaty and feminine, and chuckles, masculine and lascivious, rang through the Cambria booth at Montreal's premiere wine show, causing Shane's jaw to lock. He could leave Montreal right now and not look back.

During a full twenty-four hours in the city, although it was true that a fair portion of that time had been spent in bed, Audrey had not uttered so much as an endearment in French. Now she was flirting in the language. They had picked up more new clients today than in the Boston and New York shows combined.

He wanted to wring the neck of every man who appeared more interested in Audrey than in Cambria's Shiraz…and not because he was defending his product.

Grimly watching her pour a Riesling into the glass of a formally attired man who kept his eyes on her instead of his glass, Shane decided he wouldn't sell the bastard a bottle of wine if he were dying of thirst.

That thought soothed him only very temporarily. Then another thought came, one he liked much better. Turning away from two customers who entered the booth, he reached into his jacket pocket, withdrew his cell phone, dialed their hotel and asked to be connected to the concierge's desk.

Chapter Nineteen

It was after midnight by the time they'd stored everything they would need for the second day of the show,
grabbed a bite to eat, which proved wonderfully easy in
a town that never slept, and returned to the hotel.
Audrey's excitement over the day's success could not
be dampened. Not even by one very moody, very
unhappy-looking Aussie.

When they stepped off the elevator on their floor,
Audrey was irrepressibly reviewing the late-night
snacks they'd shared: a bagel with cream cheese for her
and a smoked meat sandwich for him, two of Montreal's
signature treats.

"That was the perfect bagel—a little chewy, a little
bready. I wonder where I could take a bagel-making
class?"

"If one exists, you'll find it."

"Hey, you do speak after midnight. I was beginning to wonder."

"You've heard me speak after midnight," he said in a dry and obvious reference to the previous night.

"I should have specified 'converse.'" They walked side by side, without touching, along the well-lit corridor. "I'm surprised you're not in a fabulous mood. This was Cambria's best night yet."

He answered without looking over or breaking stride. "Thanks to you."

Oddly, he didn't look too happy about it. "Thanks to me and you and Cambria's wines," she stated.

On they walked down the hall, and she wondered if she was destined for a good night's sleep tonight.

She didn't want one. It didn't matter that she was beyond tired. With only two nights remaining to her interlude with Shane, Audrey wanted to squeeze as much as she could from every moment.

They reached her door first, and she stopped. "This is me."

Shane didn't stop. He merely slowed and spoke over his shoulder as he pulled out his key card. "No, it's not."

She looked at the number on the door. "Yeah, it is."

"I phoned the concierge earlier this evening and had your things moved to my suite." Putting the key card in the lock, he opened his door and entered.

After several stunned seconds, she headed after him. Sure enough, her suitcase was packed and sitting neatly on a luggage rack.

"Without even telling me? That's pretty high-handed, don't you think?"

"One could interpret it that way." He yanked off his tie, tossed it over a chair and discarded his jacket the same way. Walking toward her, he began to unbutton his shirt. When it hung loose and he stood no more than a few inches away, he reached out to trail a finger from the hollow of her throat to the low, low dip of the flirtatious dress she had chosen for the wine event.

"I want to discuss this," she insisted.

"That's one option."

Quivering as Shane looped a finger where the shimmering gold material made a V between her breasts, Audrey fought her own burgeoning desire and instead gave him a stern glower. "All right, what's the other option?"

"It's going to take all night to show you." Staring at her with eyes that rivaled the blue of the Montreal skies, he murmured, "Tomorrow night, I want you to practice saying in French, 'Keep your hands to yourselves, mates. I belong to Shane.'"

As he lowered his head, her whole body began to tingle and she surrendered. "Okay," she whispered, lifting her lips to his. "But do I have to say 'mates'?"

Their passion carried them from midnight to morning. The next day they were so tired that they slept until nearly ten, and then it was Shane who set a steaming cup of coffee on the end table at Audrey's side of the bed. "Java," he tempted, his breath tickling her ear. "A nonfat mocha latte with an extra shot for the lady. You're such a girl."

Groaning, Audrey rolled to her side and jerked the

covers over her face. Shane had opened the draperies, which allowed evil Montreal sunshine to stream into the room. "Go 'way" and "morning off" were the only words she could dredge up.

Shane tugged the covers off, chuckling at her attempts to thwart him. "If I recall correctly, it was you who insisted we get up early to roller-skate along the river and then have a picnic on Mount Royal. It's past ten, so we've officially passed 'early.' If you shower in two minutes, skip breakfast and skate fast we might be able to have your picnic."

Audrey rolled onto her back, surprised by the effort it took. She was way past exhausted. A pounding headache and the feeling that vampires had drained her body of every last ounce of blood forced her to admit that burning the candle at both ends had to stop.

"Why don't we skip the roller-skating," she suggested, wondering if she'd need to skip Mount Royal as well. With a near Herculean effort, she sat up. Sometime in the night she had felt chilled to the bone and had fished through her suitcase to don a long T-shirt. Now she shivered again, wishing she'd brought pajamas. The footed variety.

Swearing when he saw her shake, Shane immediately pulled the covers back into place. He helped her adjust the pillows behind her back then sat on the bed. "You're ill. You've got shadows beneath your eyes." He felt her forehead and her cheeks. "No fever. Do you think you have a summer cold?"

She shrugged, attempting a smile on his behalf. By his own admission, his experience with Hilary had made him "clucky."

"Is your throat sore?" he asked.

It wasn't, and she knew in her gut that her symptoms were not the onset of a cold virus. But she nodded.

"You're going to stay in then," he said decisively. "I'll make another trip to the lobby, pick up a couple of cold remedies. In the meantime, you sleep. You'll be right as rain by evening."

Audrey tried to talk him into sightseeing without her, but he merely smiled and told her to close her eyes. The next time she opened them, his big, strong body was curved around her. He was on top of the covers and she lay beneath them, but the warmth and comfort penetrated to her. When she tried to rise to check the clock, his hold tightened. She could tell that the draggy, depleted feeling was still there, so she allowed herself to fall asleep again. The next time she awoke, Shane was standing in front of the mirror, tying his tie. An assortment of covered foods sat atop the table near the window and cold medicines, zinc lozenges, a thermometer and a box of tissues were piled on the table at her side.

As she pushed herself up and ran a hand through her bed-head hair, he caught sight of her in the mirror and turned. "Well, g'day, sleeping beauty. How is the patient?"

Audrey frowned. "I'm not a patient. I'm fine. Where are you going? What time is it?"

Shane came to the bed. "There's soup on the table. A sandwich, too, if your throat isn't too bad. Your job tonight is to get well. We had a beaut of a day yesterday, so I'll close the booth right on time tonight and we can have an evening in with pay-per-view. You may have picked up the same bug Hilary caught. It'll put a crimp in our sightseeing. I'd planned to surprise you with a couple of extra days in Montreal, but I can think of worse things than being alone in a room with you." He grinned and bent over the bed to give her a kiss.

"The wine show is starting and you let me sleep?" Audrey attempted to scramble from the bed, but Shane and her own weak limbs impeded her.

"Hey, don't even think about it. If you're anything like Hilary, you'll be down for the count." He reached for the carton of throat lozenges by the bed. "I was going to wake you up to take one of these, but you were sleeping soundly. Have one now."

"My throat isn't sore," she protested, quickly adding, "anymore. I must have been extra tired, that's all. My current employer is a slave driver. Keeps me up all hours of the night."

Shane wasn't amused. "It's not just fatigue, Audrey. You've been shivering on and off all day."

"I'm better now."

"All right," he said doubtfully. "Stay better." Returning the throat lozenges to the table, he picked up the zinc with C. "Take two of these and a full glass of water."

Rolling her eyes, Audrey grumbled, "Fine." She put the first lozenge in her mouth, speaking around it. "And then you'd better make yourself scarce. Since you didn't wake me up, I am going to need to do some serious hustling to make myself presentable. Consider this room my own personal spa for the next hour."

"Consider yourself out of your mind if you think I'm going to let you work." He held up a hand when she started to argue. "By evening the first day, Hil was coughing and sneezing. You won't draw people to the booth tonight. You'll keep them away in droves." To soften the impact of his words, he stroked his knuckles gently down her cheek. "You're still pale, sweetheart. You've lost weight this past week, too." He frowned suddenly. "Have you been feeling ill all week?"

Audrey would have liked nothing better at that moment than to have the mother of all colds. Fear settled upon her like an icy, bony hand. Dr. McFarland had cautioned her to phone immediately if she began to have more symptoms. Her nervous glance took in the table laden with what appeared to be all the medicines a hotel gift shop was apt to stock. Near the window her late lunch beckoned, and seated beside her, Shane looked concerned and…loving.

For an instant, reality fell away, and in the space between truth and denial a steady, quiet calm descended. It took her a moment to identify it. Trust. For the space of a few breaths, she trusted Shane to love her no matter where they were, no matter what was happening in the present or would happen in the future. She trusted him to love her without resentment and without regrets.

It felt like floating—weightless and liquid and gentle. Audrey thought she could go through anything in life with that feeling inside her, but in the blink of an eye it evaporated, leaving the nauseatingly hollow sensation of her stomach dropping.

"Audrey," Shane persisted, "have you felt ill all week?"

She shook her head, making the nervous queasiness worse. She had spent years acting tough, unconcerned, even arrogant. Now she felt vulnerable and defenseless, a once-bold and independent eagle plucked until it felt like a chicken.

She loved Shane. She needed and wanted him. Yet in some cruel way she failed to understand, the love that strengthened others made her feel powerless and afraid. The closer she got to a real life with him, the more she experienced an agonizing dread.

Standing and crossing to the other side of the king-size bed, Shane reached for the phone. "I'm calling the concierge. You're going to see a doctor."

The pronouncement jolted Audrey. "No, I'm not!"

His eyes narrowed. He shook his head, slowly. "Why do you have to be so bloody stubborn? Let me take care of you."

Temptation swelled inside her, sweet and terrifying. Once, long ago, she had been watched over, cared for. She had felt safe regardless of the circumstances. When that care was ripped away, she had been left with an ache more awful than any illness.

"I don't need anyone to take care of me." The denial sounded sharp, like the yip of a small, scared dog. "I don't want to be taken care of."

"Everyone needs it sometimes, sweet—"

"No!" Audrey scrambled off the bed, to the side opposite Shane. She felt wobbly on legs that hadn't hit the floor all day except to carry her once to the bathroom. Beneath her T-shirt, her heart beat like a kettledrum. "Some people need to be taken care of," came her shaky disavowal as heat flushed her cheeks, "and other people love to do it, because it makes them feel good about themselves. I don't need your concern. If taking over Hilary's life hasn't given you 'meaning,' then find another invalid. I'm not available."

The awful accusation charged the air with something dark and barbed. Audrey knew she was being unfair, but the words rose from an old untended well of fear inside her. The closer she came to trusting Shane completely, the more frightened she became, as if she were trying to outrun a tidal wave. She wanted distance between them, needed it.

Shane's grip on the telephone tightened, but he replaced the receiver with eerie control.

She expected a volley as arch and unforgiving as the grenade she'd lobbed at him. God knew she deserved one.

Instead, Shane's eyes widened as if he'd had a realization, one that left him more disgusted with himself than with her. "Obviously I don't listen as well as I thought. You've been saying from the beginning that this is temporary for you. Fun." A grim, humorless smile touched his lips. "I heard you this time."

Audrey did not wait for Shane to return from the wine show that night so she could say goodbye. She left for the airport as soon as she'd showered and packed. Shane had been right: they'd done a terrific business the night before. From that perspective, Montreal was already a success. He would be able to handle the booth without her. And there was nothing she could say, nothing at all to repair the damage she had done to their relationship. Unless perhaps she told the truth.

She was tired still and shaky from lack of food when she entered the airport, but she didn't want to stop to eat until after she'd been to the reservations desk. Even if she had to sleep sitting up in a chair while she waited for her flight, at least she was on her way to the one place that might help her make sense of her tangled, knotted emotions. Questions burned in her mind, and the only person who could answer them had not been seen or heard from in over a decade.

Informing the agent that she needed the next available flight out, Audrey handed over her credit card and purchased a one-way ticket. To California.

Laguna Niguel was a community devoted to beauty, cleanliness and the rich, or at least the rich at heart. Real estate had doubtlessly made fortunes for the lucky agents whose careers had been well-timed. Even now, post–real-estate boom, Audrey guessed that the sale of only one or two choice properties would feather a bank account quite nicely.

Walking into the luxurious office of Rumson-Helio Real Estate confirmed the impression. "I'm here to see Gwen Helio." Heart pounding, she announced herself to the receptionist. "I have an appointment."

The sunny southern California blonde smiled professionally. "Your name?"

"Lea Cambria." Audrey fibbed, hoping Hilary wouldn't mind her borrowing the last name.

The receptionist checked the large appointment book in front of her. "Mrs. Helio is showing a home and running a bit late. You're welcome to wait in her office, if you'd like to follow me."

Audrey did want to wait in *Mrs.* Helio's office. She

followed the well-dressed young woman, hoping she appeared far more composed than she felt.

They stepped into a room appointed with a gorgeous cherrywood desk, overstuffed chairs upholstered in an elegant ivory suede that Audrey would be afraid to sit on in her usual attire, and a built-in cabinet sparsely filled with framed photos and artwork from around the globe.

After offering Audrey something to drink, the receptionist left, closing the door with a soft click.

Audrey stood still, hardly daring to move or breathe. This was as close as she had come to her mother in over a decade.

The room smelled like Gwen. Not the way she had smelled years ago—of the lavender and white ginger oils she had mixed—but the way Audrey imagined she smelled now: expensive and sophisticated.

Mama, you've moved up in the world.

The private investigator Audrey had hired six months ago had provided a photo of Gwen walking toward her office, sporting a beveled blond pageboy, large sunglasses and heels that must have clicked sharply on the pavement, so different from the thirty-one-year-old woman who had worn sundresses and sandals and her sun-streaked brown hair in a ponytail.

From the file, Audrey had discovered her mother's new name and her place of business. That and the photo were the only bits of information for which she had asked. She'd been too afraid to see anything more.

Now though, she instructed herself to move, to take advantage of this opportunity to explore her mother's life, her new life, before she met Gwen face-to-face.

Starting with the desk, Audrey noted several framed photos. She reached out a hand then pulled it back abruptly, chills racing up her arms. Generally people kept photos of family on their desks.

For nearly twelve years, Audrey had ached to ask her mother why she had left without any warning. Without taking Audrey with her. Her stomach had twisted continually with the need to know whether Gwen was aware her daughter had gotten sick again and, if so, why she hadn't returned. Whose photos were on this desk? Would there be one of Audrey?

There had been endless days during chemo when Audrey had refused to cry or complain one bit, thinking that somehow her mother would find out how brave and strong she had become. She had tried not to throw up until the very last second and then she had taken care of herself. If she didn't cry, if Gwen didn't have to hold her while she moaned or was smelly, then maybe…

There had come the day, of course, when it had been easier by far for Audrey to believe that she no longer cared about Gwen, no longer needed her.

A convenient lie.

Slowly she reached for one of the photos, her fingers trembling as they touched the silver frame. She turned it toward her, and her breath caught like a great hiccup.

Taken on a pristine stretch of beach, the photo showed her mother and a man Audrey assumed was Mr. Helio—tall, dark-haired, roughly Gwen's age. The couple was sitting on the sand. Clowning for the camera in front of them were two children, a boy and a girl. The children shared the dark hair of their father and their mother's fine features. Gwen's hand rested on the shoulder of the girl, whom Audrey guessed to be about eight years old.

Audrey wanted to be philosophical. She had always wondered if Gwen had had more children. Until now, however, she had not fully appreciated the difference between wondering and knowing.

You should leave.

The thought came in a flash and with it the increased heart rate of someone prepared to flee. She had no chance to find out whether she would truly run or not; the doorknob turned and in walked the woman whose Valentine's cards had once been addressed, "To the BEST mom on PLANET EARTH. Love you 4-ever, Audrey."

In an ivory skirt and matching silk shell, the sophisticate before Audrey bore little resemblance to the young mother she had known, and Audrey was glad she had worn one of her new outfits.

She could see that Gwen did not recognize her right away—one fantasy shot to hell. To her, the young woman holding one of her personal photos was merely a potential client with questionable manners.

"I'm so sorry to have kept you waiting, Ms. Cambria. I was showing a property along the coast highway. A lovely place, if you don't mind the traffic."

With a professionally gracious smile, she crossed to Audrey and extended her hand. Foolishly, Audrey held out the photo instead of giving Gwen her own hand to shake. After a moment's surprise, Gwen laughed to cover the awkwardness. "My family. We live and play in Laguna Niguel, as well as do most of our business here. So if you're in the market for a local property—"

"I'm not," Audrey interrupted.

Gwen tilted her head, her blond hair brushing her shoulder. "Are you selling your home then, Ms. Cambria?"

Audrey shook her head. Her mouth felt horribly dry. "I'm not selling anything. And my name isn't Cambria."

Gwen glanced down at the photo, replacing it before she looked up again, her brows drawn together. Turning away from Audrey, she crossed to the door, closing it firmly. When she looked back, her gaze swept her visitor, returning to Audrey's face with a searching expression. Slowly her mother nodded, chest rising on a deeply drawn breath. "My goodness," she said quietly. "I should have noticed your eyes right away. You look beautiful."

Audrey swallowed hard. A strange thing, to want to sob because her mother remembered her eyes. Reigning in her emotions, Audrey said, "I'm sorry I lied about my name. I wasn't sure you would see me."

Without denying or confirming that impression, Gwen offered, "Would you like to sit down?"

Audrey took one of the two chairs in front of the desk. After a moment's hesitation, Gwen pulled out the chair next to her and sat so they were facing. "If there's a graceful way to begin, I'm not sure what it is," she admitted with a strained, apologetic smile.

Audrey didn't know, either, so she leaped into the silence. "Dad died last year."

Gwen's eyes flared with surprise. "I'm sorry. That must have been very difficult for you."

So many emotions tried to squeeze into Audrey's chest at once. Anger, elation, disappointment, hope— she didn't know what to feel, and Gwen wasn't helping. She hadn't assumed her mother was still in love with the husband she had left, but Audrey still saw the three of them as they had been—a family. News of Henry's death didn't seem to affect Gwen personally.

"You wrote me a letter before you left. Do you remember? You said you hoped that someday I'd under-stand." Audrey tried to keep accusation out of her voice as she referred to the brief note her mother had penned, informing Audrey and Henry that she was leaving, but neglecting to explain…a damn thing. "I think 'someday' is here, but I still don't understand. Was it him?" Audrey gestured to the photo she'd picked up. "Mr. Helio. Is he the reason—"

She broke off as her mother shook her head. "I didn't meet Dustin for a couple of years. There wasn't another man when I left." She glanced down at perfectly mani-cured nails. "I suppose my decision would be easier to understand if there had been another man." When she made eye contact again, her expression was more guarded. "Your father was quite a bit older than I, Audrey. He knew what he wanted in life. I was only nineteen when I had you. That was too young. I always hoped you would wait to marry, have children." She raised a brow, asking the question.

"I'm still single," Audrey confirmed, her voice raspy. *Because I'd rather throw love away than be a burden to anyone. I'd rather be alone than need someone and feel like I want to die when they walk away.*

She rose, unable to sit still. Unable to sit across from the woman who should have stuck around or written a damn letter every once in a while if she'd wanted to give her daughter life lessons.

Wrapping her arms around her middle, Audrey crossed to the window and breathed, trying to calm the turmoil inside her. *Not gonna happen.*

"You may have been nineteen when you had me," she said, and this time she sounded accusing as hell, "but you were thirty-one when you left." She looked over her shoulder. "The kids in that photo…they're what? Seven? Eight?"

"Tyler is six. Emilia is eight."

"It didn't take you too long to decide you were ready for more kids. Sorry if I can't buy immaturity as the excuse for leaving your first family."

Gwen's chin lifted. Her still taut jaw tensed. She rose regally, and Audrey thought she had blown it, that she was going to be kicked out of the office and out of her mother's life again before she'd gotten any real answers at all. She wondered if she would cry or leave with dignity, or whether she should open the office door and shout to everyone within earshot that she was perfect Gwen's very imperfect daughter. She had told herself that mostly what she wanted was information, a couple of the puzzle pieces that had been missing for so long. But in her heart of hearts, hadn't she yearned for a reunion worthy of an *Oprah* segment?

Gwen approached until she stood very close to her daughter. Staring directly into Audrey's eyes, she said with a voice that wavered only slightly, "I wasn't strong enough to stay, Audrey. If you want the truth, that's it. It all got to be too much—a marriage that had never worked, illness. Living at the hospital or in doctors' offices."

Tears—of shame, of guilt, of fear—clogged Audrey's throat. "It was too hard? I was too hard to take care of?" She sounded young, pathetic, and she nearly hated herself for asking the question out loud.

"Not you. That life. Never knowing what was going to happen. The constant threat of more trouble, even after everything seemed to be fine. Never being able to plan...a thing. Your father was so much better at it than I. I stayed until you were in remission, and then I left, because I thought I would go crazy if I didn't. I had no idea who I was. I'd never given myself the chance to find out."

Audrey broke eye contact, confusion and guilt making it hard to think. Her mother had hated her life. How did it work in other families? How did the good outweigh the bad so that even if you needed to "find" yourself, you didn't leave your daughter to do it?

Blinking to hold back tears, she let her gaze dart around the room to the expensive furniture, the tasteful art, the clothes that wouldn't wilt even in hundred-degree weather. This was her mother—all this perfection.

Then Audrey glanced down at herself. She didn't want to wear a crisp linen dress. She missed her jeans. She missed her father. She missed the mother who had wrapped her in shawls and sat on a floral sofa with her to watch *I Love Lucy* reruns. How perfect would she have to have been to keep that? How perfect to capture that comfort again?

"*Thoroughbreds race and draft horses haul.*" Her

father's calm voice cut through the chatter in her brain. *"If they tried to do each other's job, not a lick of work would get done."*

That had been Henry's response the year she'd worn the wig to make Robbie Preston notice her. In other words, *To thine own self be true.* It was a lot easier if you liked thine own self.

Henry had tried to teach her to value herself as he had valued her—steadfastly, no matter what. Bald and cranky, brave and strong—she had been the apple of his eye, always. But Gwen's lessons had packed the greater wallop.

Because you let them. Because you were just a scared kid.

In front of Audrey, Gwen shifted nervously, her glance moving from Audrey to the photo of her new family.

Memories of the way her mother had once rubbed her temples with lavender oil came rushing back.

"You took good care of me when I was sick," Audrey told Gwen in a choked voice, but she couldn't say "Mom."

Gwen looked up. Tears had gathered in her eyes. Taking another liberty, Audrey walked around the desk to see the other photos, one a wedding shot of Gwen and her husband, the other a two-shot of Tyler and Emilia— her half brother and sister. They were posed around a gorgeous Christmas tree, their clothes and hair and smiles…well, perfect. There were no pictures of the past.

"Are they healthy?" The question popped out before Audrey could reconsider.

There was a pause. She found herself relieved when Gwen answered, "Yes."

Another silence followed, and Audrey realized she

was waiting for a question in return. She studied Gwen, seeing the query in her eyes, watching the artfully colored lips part to voice the words, *Are you?* Then she saw her mother come to a decision. Gwen closed her mouth again and kept it closed, the question unasked, the information unwanted.

"I can't tell Dustin about my past," she said, her lips barely moving, her guilt nearly palpable. "We...I'm on the school board. He's running for city council. I wouldn't know what to tell him...or anyone. They wouldn't understand."

Resentment filled Audrey to the brim. *I know the feeling.*

But in the next moment, she thought of Shane instead of Gwen. Shane, who found purpose and meaning not in someone else's illness, as she had so wrongfully accused him, but in loving through thick and thin.

She had spent the past dozen years afraid to believe she could be loved in sickness and in health when in reality, it had never been about her. She would be loved according to the capacity of the person doing the loving. And her own capacity to take it in.

She had been a pretender for so long. *Live for today; ignore tomorrow. Don't ask; don't tell. I don't need anyone to take care of me...*

She'd steeped herself in more muck than any horse stabled at Quest.

Suddenly the truth thundered through her brain like dozens of hooves racing toward the finish line. *Choice.* In every circumstance—sick or well, loved or abandoned—she had a choice. She hadn't seen it then.

Gwen had no idea that Audrey had relapsed after she'd left. She wouldn't have come home, anyway.

Audrey could choose to see that as somebody's fault—her own, Gwen's, God's. Or, she could see it as a devastating weakness, a decision she, Audrey, would never make, not in a million years, if someone she loved needed her.

She could focus on how good it felt to love her father or how rotten it was to miss a mom. She could walk toward love or live in grief. Her choice.

At once, Audrey knew she wanted to go home. She looked at her mother's beautiful face and realized she would never seek Gwen out again. There would be questions left unasked, the answers incapable of erasing life's uncertainties, anyway.

She had lived for so long in the shadow of Gwen's decisions rather than the sunlight of her own.

Sunlight, she decided now, firmly, vehemently. *I choose summer.*

Chapter Twenty

Dr. Carmen McFarland's waiting room was designed to feel homey and comforting. She kept the antiqued sideboard stocked with tea, china cups and stacks of *Health* and *O* magazines. The furniture was upholstered in cozy chenille.

Seated on the loveseat closest to the reception desk, Audrey tried to let the waiting room's inherent normalcy soothe her nerves. No matter how upbeat she had tried to remain over the past week, there had been precious few moments during which she'd forgotten the importance of this appointment. One week ago, she had undergone outpatient surgery to biopsy an enlarged lymph node. Today, Carmen would deliver the results of that and other tests intended to make sense of the symptoms Audrey had been suffering for the past several months.

Audrey had been in the waiting room for fifteen minutes, and her palms were starting to sweat. She'd have wiped them on her jeans, but the women seated on either side of her were holding her hands.

To her left, Jenna squeezed her fingers reassuringly; to her right, Melanie asked, "Ready for some tea?"

"No, thanks. I'm too nervous to drink it." She smiled at the two friends who had been such a wonderful support to her since she'd returned from California.

Instead of going through the surgery on her own, Audrey had gathered all her courage and confided in the Prestons. The moment she had asked for help, she had gotten it, abundantly. They had accompanied her to the hospital for her surgery, insisted she stay in the big house for a couple of nights and then took for granted that she would need company on her return visit to the doctor.

Audrey and Melanie had hung out in the library or on the patio at night, chatting about a number of things—Melanie's enthusiasm for Something to Talk About, her anger over the stress her family was suffering at the hands of the gossip-hungry media, and Audrey's feelings for Shane. Never before had Audrey been as open. Never before had she felt so much was at stake.

She'd had time to evaluate her feelings for Shane and she knew she loved him. She also knew that she had hurt him and destroyed the first sweet buds of their relationship. She didn't know if he would give her another chance—or whether life would. Shane had already returned to Australia with Hilary; she hadn't spoken to him since Montreal, and she'd decided—against Melanie's advice—not to tell him about the biopsy. She would call him eventually. She wanted to tell him the truth behind her rotten behavior, and she needed to apologize, but there was more she had to tell him—like the fact that she was unlikely to bear children—and she ached to do it without the backdrop of a current illness. She'd behaved abominably; she wanted to bring him good news, not involve him in more drama. And she didn't want him to stay out of guilt.

"I hope they're not running too late," Audrey murmured, unable to contain her nervousness and glad that for the first time in a long, long while she felt no need to pretend. She heard the women on either side of her murmur something, but failed to catch the words, for at that moment, the door leading into the doctor's office opened, and a wheelchair rolled across the threshold.

"Oh, aces! We're not late." Hilary smiled at Audrey, who was too shocked to do more than stare.

Her pulse skittered as she waited to see who was holding the door. When Shane walked into the waiting area, Audrey forgot why she was there. She forgot whom she was with or that she was concerned about a thing. For a rare, precious moment, all she knew was that Shane was back, and the world was right.

He approached the couch, where the three women sat, but his eyes were all for Audrey.

Melanie and Jenna rose to greet Hilary, creating space for Shane to sit beside Audrey. "I'd have been here sooner," he said, "but Jenna only phoned two days ago. Communications between the U.S. and Australia have been a bit sluggish." He took her hand. "You had surgery and didn't tell me. Obviously I can't let you out of my sight." Raising her hand, he brought it to his lips for a soft and lingering kiss. "I've missed you like the very devil."

"I've missed you, too," she admitted on a whisper. Oh, how she had missed him. "I was going to tell you about…all this. I just wanted to wait until…until I knew what to tell you."

"There's only one thing I want to hear, you sweet, stubborn nitwit." He cupped her jaw, drawing her close. "In the whole bloody language there are only three words that explain every crazy decision any man or woman has ever made. Say them. All the rest is details, sweetheart."

Audrey searched his eyes, aware of their audience and of the fear that still gurgled in her tummy. How difficult could three little words be? It was high time to retire her "Seize the day" philosophy in favor of something more farsighted—like someday looking back at her life and knowing she had made it through thick and thin, sickness and health, boredom and joy with one person. That would be the sexiest, craziest, sweetest thing of all.

She reached up to take Shane's face between her hands, and she didn't mind who heard them, really, as she stared into his eyes with all the truth in her heart pouring out.

"Shane Preston, I love you. I want to be with you always, if you'll take me as I am. I had some crazy idea that my doctor would say this was all a false alarm and that's when I'd come to you, so we could start on more equal footing. There's so much I still have to tell you—"

Shane pulled her in for a kiss that made everyone in

the waiting room lower their magazines in favor of staring. The receptionist buzzed the examining room to tell Dr. McFarland that she might not want to miss this.

When the kiss broke, Shane held Audrey's face so she had to look directly into his eyes when he told her, "There is nothing, *nothing* you can tell me to change the way I feel. But I'm a man who plans ahead, which you'll have to deal with, so rule one, full disclosure from now on. I don't want to have to find out from my cousin that you love me. Or that you've fought cancer. Or that you've had surgery I didn't know about."

Audrey had to agree before Shane would release her face so she could turn toward the three women attempting to slink off toward the restrooms. "Hold it!" she called. "Hilary, I didn't tell you about the surgery. And I've only told one person that I'm in love with Shane, so— Melanie! You didn't. I swore you to secrecy!"

Melanie looked slightly shamefaced. "I didn't think you meant my mom. You're like a daughter to her." She glanced sideways at Jenna. "And I didn't think she'd tell anyone."

That last part was so blatantly a lie, Audrey didn't bother to dignify it. She merely arched a brow at Jenna.

The older woman shrugged. "I may have mentioned something to Hilary. In passing. She's family now. And I did point out that it was private information and that if you wanted to share it with Shane, you would have to do so in your own time. No matter how *long* that took."

All eyes turned toward Hilary, dressed in a vibrant skirt in hues of blue with a matching summer top. No hiding for her. Pushing manicured fingers through the thick mink hair she wore loose and flowing, she rolled her eyes at the small crowd waiting to discover if she'd ratted out her friend. "Well, what do you think?" she purred, about as recalcitrant as a cat who had a mouse in its mouth.

Carmen's nurse appeared at that moment, weaving around the cluster of people in their modest waiting room, and told Audrey that the doctor was ready to see her.

Audrey felt a shiver run through her then felt Shane take her arm as they stood. As they started after the nurse, he pulled her close and whispered for her ears only, "Before I forget—I love you, too. I want to marry you—when you're ready—so I bought you a small engagement present to seal the deal."

Audrey stepped back to look at him, a hairsbreadth from flinging her arms around him and screaming. He gave her another kiss, murmured, "We'll talk more later, without the peanut gallery."

As everyone belonging to Audrey's party made to follow the nurse, she looked a bit uncomfortable and stopped to ask, "Who will actually be in the room with Audrey and Dr. McFarland?"

"That would be all of us," Hilary informed the nurse, her gracious tone laced with a thread of steel. She was getting really good at that.

The nurse frowned, but they heard her mutter, "I'll bring in extra chairs," as they squeezed into the room.

Carmen, a fit middle-aged woman who had been Audrey's primary physician for several years, entered the room before her nurse returned. "Oh, my," she said, seeing that her office was filled to capacity. Assured that those who were standing were perfectly happy to do so, she greeted Audrey with a hug. Continuing around to the chair behind her desk, she sat across from Audrey and Shane, opened a folder on her desk, glanced through a couple of lab printouts and formed a steeple under her chin with her fingers.

"So. You've had some disturbing symptoms, my dear, particularly given your history. Instead of testing one thing at a time, we decided to proceed with a biopsy as well as blood tests to check for thyroid and autoimmune disorder." She paused. "We did find several things we'd rather not see in someone so young. And a couple labs that suggest responsibility for your symptoms of coldness, fatigue and the swollen nodes."

Shane's hand gripped Audrey's. The tension in the room seemed to mount with each of Carmen's words. Audrey wondered if she alone was feeling peaceful. Life. On life's terms. She'd fought hard before to live, and she could do it again, especially with a heart full of reasons. And if she couldn't have kids…there were different ways to build the family she knew Shane wanted. The family she wanted, too.

She relaxed her fingers against his, hoping to communicate that they would be okay.

"All right, Doc. What have I got?"

"A very sluggish thyroid, for one thing. That's responsible for at least some of your fatigue and the coldness you've been feeling, especially in your extremities. It's not unheard of to develop thyroid issues soon after a period of grief, which seems to upset the endocrine system. In hypothyroidism, we expect to see weight gain, but you appear to be losing weight. That happens rarely, but again it's not unheard of. We can correct the imbalance with a simple medication."

She referred back to her notes. "Of a little more concern is your white cell count. It's low. That means you could have trouble kicking out a virus. When we checked, your titers were up, indicating that a virus had taken hold at some point and is still in your body. That accounts for the swollen nodes."

Audrey blinked. "A virus. But not…cancer."

Carmen shook her head. "Not cancer. The lymph node we sampled was benign." While Audrey was enveloped in hugs, the doctor went on. "A weakened immune system is still nothing to sneeze at, Audrey—pardon the pun. It's a warning sign to fix whatever is going on. Your body needs to be strong enough to fight a virus so it doesn't turn into a cornucopia of symptoms. How have you been taking care of yourself lately? Because I have to tell you, your cholesterol levels are too high for someone your age." She checked her notes again and muttered, "They're too high for someone *my* age. And your blood sugar is up. At your last checkup we talked about adding more whole grains and veggies to your diet and minimizing sweets. Have you done that?"

Audrey didn't have a chance to reply. The three women around her began regaling the physician with Audrey's dietary indiscretions. They were ratting her out to her own doctor. And Carmen was shaking her head and making notes.

Beside her, Shane spoke below the cacophony of voices. "It's time for me to give you your engagement gift."

Audrey threw him a look of heartfelt irony. "Chocolate?"

Shane cleared his throat. "Yeah, those days are gone. At least until we know you have the immune system of a Hunza." He reached into his jacket pocket, withdrawing an envelope. Opening it, he handed her the contents. "You might like this even better."

Quickly, she scanned a written statement of intention to transfer ownership of the Thoroughbred Biding Her Time from Thomas Preston to Audrey Griffin.

Her gaze swung to Shane's. "But, I don't understand. How did you know—"

"I've seen her bring Fluffernutters to the stable for lunch." Melanie was standing over Carmen now, who was writing furiously on Audrey's file and pursing her lips. "And she washes them down with fruit punch."

"I would be more than happy to stock her refrigerator, and we would love for her to take more meals with us," Jenna offered to the doctor's nodding approval.

"Better not let her out of your sight for a while, though," Hilary pitched in. "I could describe meals when we were on our trip that would curl your hair." She blithely overlooked the day she'd introduced Audrey to Australian chocolate bikkies.

"Let me guess." Audrey returned her attention to Shane and the gift he'd given her. "You knew how I felt about Biding Her Time, because Melanie told Jenna."

He nodded, to his credit keeping a straight face. "I think Jenna mentioned something to Hilary. In passing."

"And Hilary—"

Shane grinned. "What do you think?" Incapable of

waiting a moment longer to begin the series of kisses he intended to continue far into the evening, he went ahead and got started on her arm. Audrey grinned back, shivering in a good way as he touched his lips—and, ooh, his tongue—to the inside of her wrist.

"Shane, for heaven's sake, wait five minutes until you can take it outside." Hilary reached over and whacked him on the shoulder with a *Five A Day For Better Health* pamphlet. "The doctor wants to know if you'll be able to support good self-care for Audrey if she moves to Australia. She'll have to comply with her medication and get exercise and rest, and she positively has to eat food that once touched soil, not bags and bags of things that glow in the dark. If you're going to be too easy on her—"

With his integrity and sense of purpose called into question, Audrey feared she wouldn't get any more kisses for a while. "Of course I'm going to be diligent about her diet!" Shane exclaimed, turning his attention to Hilary. "We'll clear the house of any food that would undermine…"

Oh, brother. While the others argued her nutrition plan, Audrey toyed briefly with the notion of escaping for a thick-crust pepperoni pizza, then sighed and resigned herself to something very green and filled with sprouts.

Folding the paper that disclosed her engagement present, she hoped Biding Her Time would enjoy living in Australia.

With a smile, she blew a kiss to her father, wishing he could be here to see that she was amply taken care of, thoroughly in love, and surrounded by family.

"Hey, guys…guys!" She interrupted a burgeoning debate about whether Vegemite was a health food, and the cluster of people with her best interests at heart turned to look at her. "Anybody want to go out for a veggie burger?"

Already she felt better than she had in weeks… months… maybe years. And she was so, so ready to take a big fat bite out of life.

Grinning, she announced, "I don't know about you all, but I'm absolutely starving."

* * * * *

Thoroughbred Legacy

The purse is set and the stakes are high…
Romance, Scandal and Glamour set in the
exhilarating world of horse-racing!

The Legacy Continues with Book #3

PICTURE OF PERFECTION

by Kristin Gabriel

Veterinarian Carter Phillips is mystified about a scandal
surrounding prize-winning horse Leopold's Legacy—and he thinks
artist Gillian Cameron is just the person to give him answers.
Gillian knows she can't trust Carter's agenda, since it could
compromise the horse's future and that of her family. So why does
she find herself wanting to trust him with a mystery of her own?

Look for PICTURE OF PERFECTION
in July 2008 wherever books are sold.

TL19916

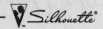

SPECIAL EDITION

A late-night walk on the beach resulted
in Trevor Marlowe's heroic rescue of a
drowning woman. He took the amnesia
victim in and dubbed her Venus, for the
goddess who'd emerged from the sea.
It looked as if she might be his goddess of
love, too…until her former fiancé showed
up on Trevor's doorstep.

Don't miss

THE BRIDE WITH NO NAME

by *USA TODAY* bestselling author
MARIE FERRARELLA

*Available August
wherever you buy books.*

REQUEST YOUR FREE BOOKS!
2 FREE NOVELS PLUS 2 FREE GIFTS!

SPECIAL EDITION®
Life, Love and Family!

SPECIAL EDITION™

NEW YORK TIMES BESTSELLING AUTHOR

DIANA PALMER

A brand-new Long, Tall Texans novel

HEART OF STONE

Feeling unwanted and unloved, Keely returns to Jacobsville and to Boone Sinclair, a rancher troubled by his own past. Boone has always seemed reserved, but now Keely discovers a sensuality with him that quickly turns to love. Can they each see past their own scars to let love in?

Available September 2008
wherever you buy books.